Mr. Cepeda stopped in front of an exhibit of leopards from Asia. "Listen," he said, lowering his voice. "There's something I forgot to tell you."

Already I was scared, just from his tone of voice.

"I forgot to tell you about a really weird and scary legend.

"According to the legend, life is very hard for the creatures and the people in these museum exhibits, because they have to stay so still all year round.

"On Halloween night," he went on, "at the stroke of midnight, the exhibits all come to life. They stretch and roam around." He smiled. "Do I need to remind any of you that tonight is Halloween night?"

JOIN THE TEAM!

Do you watch GHOSTWRITER on PBS? Then you know that when you read and write to solve a mystery or unravel a puzzle, you're using the same smarts and skills the Ghostwriter Team uses.

We hope you'll join the team and read along to help solve the mysterious and puzzling goings-on in all of the GHOSTWRITER books!

NIGHT
OF THE LIVING
CAVEMEN

Ghostwriter™

NIGHT
OF THE LIVING
CAVEMEN

by **Eric Weiner**
Illustrated by Phil Franké

A Children's Television Workshop Book

Bantam Books
New York Toronto London Sydney Auckland

NIGHT OF THE LIVING CAVEMEN
A Bantam Book/September 1995
This novel is a work of fiction. Any references or similarities to real people, events,
establishments, organizations, or locales are intended only to give the fiction a sense of reality
and authenticity.

Ghostwriter, **Ghost**writer and ● are
trademarks of Children's Television Workshop.
All rights reserved. Used under authorization.

Thanks to **SEGA** and the **SEGA FOUNDATION**
and to others who helped pay for GHOSTWRITER: public
television viewers, The Pew Charitable Trusts, the
Corporation for Public Broadcasting,
the Arthur Vining Davis Foundations,
the *Nike* Just Do It Fund, the John S. and James L. Knight
Foundation, and Children's Television Workshop.

Written by Eric Weiner
Interior illustrations by Phil Franké
Cover design by Marietta Anastassatos
Cover photo of caveman: UPI/Bettmann Archives

ISBN 0-553-48292-0
Published simultaneously in the United States and Canada

Bantam Books are published by Bantam Books, a division of Bantam Doubleday Dell Publishing
Group, Inc. Its trademark, consisting of the words "Bantam Books" and the portrayal of a
rooster, is registered in U.S. Patent and Trademark Office and in other countries. Marca
Registrada. Bantam Books, 1540 Broadway, New York, New York 10036.

PRINTED IN THE UNITED STATES OF AMERICA
OPM   0 9 8 7 6 5 4 3 2 1

NIGHT
OF THE LIVING
CAVEMEN

chapter
one

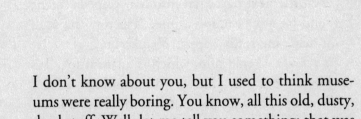

I don't know about you, but I used to think museums were really boring. You know, all this old, dusty, dead stuff. Well, let me tell you something: that was before I slept in one. That was before I got attacked by cavemen with ancient stone axes! That was before I—

But I'm getting ahead of myself. Before I start telling you all the wild and creepy things that happened to me in the museum, I should explain how I came to sleep there in the first place.

Two weeks ago at assembly, my science teacher, Mr. Cepeda, made an announcement. He said the Natural History Museum of New York had started this special program called "Sleepover Science." The idea was for schoolkids to camp out in the museum overnight. That way they could see all the exhibits without having to push through crowds of tourists.

Mr. Cepeda said he was going to put a sign-up sheet for the trip to Manhattan on the door of his science lab.

I like to think of myself as a pretty smart kid. But I started school in Puerto Rico, not Brooklyn. Doing all my schoolwork in English is hard. I figured there was no way I was going to sign up for *extra* school. I didn't even go near that sign-up list.

Then the next day I ran into Mr. Cepeda in the hall and he was beaming at me. "Hector," he said, "you made me really happy. Thank you."

"De nada," I told him, which is Spanish for "It's nothing." "But, uh, what are you thanking me for?"

"You signed up for the museum trip! I never knew you were so interested in science."

What I should have said was "I'm not." Or "What are you talking about?" Something like that. But the thing was, I had never seen Mr. Cepeda in such a good mood.

Mr. Cepeda is a big burly Latino guy with this very soft voice. Most of the time he looks pretty sad, probably because a lot of the kids in our school don't pay much attention to his classes. Right now he looked so happy, I felt like I couldn't disappoint him. So I said, "Well, you know, that museum trip sounded like it was worth checking out."

Mr. Cepeda clapped me on the back. "Hector, my man, you won't be sorry. You wait and see. This trip is going to be totally thrilling!"

At the time neither one of us had any idea how right he was.

As soon as Mr. C. walked away, I heard giggling. I spun around and there was Casey.

Casey Austin is eight. Her real name is Cassandra, but no one ever calls her that except teachers when she gets them really mad. Casey's a cousin of another friend of mine, Jamal Jenkins. She's from Detroit, but her mother has a bad drinking problem. So she's been staying at Jamal's house. She's a good kid and tough, too—more like a boy than a girl. But she loves to play practical jokes and ask dumb riddles and if you ask me, she giggles way too much.

She was giggling right now, like I said.

And then I heard *more* giggling. I turned around the other way, and there was Gaby.

Gaby Fernandez is ten. She's my friend Alex's younger sister and one of the founding members of our Ghostwriter Team. (I'll explain more about that in a minute.) She's also this really great person who's lots of fun to be around. Especially when Alex *isn't* around. When the two of them are together it's bicker, bicker, bicker. You know how it is with brothers and sisters.

Anyway, the way Casey and Gaby were laughing, it didn't take me long to figure out the mystery.

"You signed my name," I said, shaking my head. "You signed me up for the trip!"

Casey had both hands over her mouth, she was giggling so hard.

"I never knew you were so interested in science," Gaby said, doing a pretty good imitation of Mr. Cepeda. She poked me in the ribs.

I wasn't too mad. I knew Gaby and Casey were already signed up for the trip. If they were going, how bad could it be?

I live in Fort Greene, Brooklyn, which most people will tell you is not the richest neighborhood in the world. I don't get to make trips across the river into Manhattan too often. And besides, there was another event coming up that I was looking forward to so much, I didn't really care what happened in between.

It was only two weeks until Halloween. Alex and I had gotten permission from our parents to march in a special midnight Halloween parade in Manhattan. Before the parade, we were going to go trick-or-treating and rack up a whole mess of candy.

I like candy as much as the next kid. But at the moment I had an extra-special reason for wanting loads of the stuff. This past summer I started collecting candy bar wrappers. I already had more than thirty different wrappers. I figured on Halloween I could double my collection in one night!

That week I started working on a caveman costume, making a papier-mâché mask and a fake bearskin out of a brown bathmat. Every morning when

I woke up, the first thing I'd do was run to look at the costume and do more work on it before school. I couldn't think about anything else.

So what happened?

On the day of our museum trip, Mr. Cepeda got the stomach flu. He got permission from the museum to reschedule the outing—for when?

Halloween night, of course.

Have you ever noticed how that always happens? You can go for weeks when nothing happens in your life. And then three or four special things all take place at the exact same minute and you have to miss most of them.

So on Halloween night, instead of wearing my cool caveman costume, I was wearing my usual school clothes. Plus a backpack. And I was lugging an old, ratty, brown sleeping bag my mom borrowed from a neighbor of ours in the projects.

The projects are these big apartment buildings that the city built. Mostly I don't mind living there. We have a playground right in front of my building with lots of handball courts. And there are always tons of kids running around for me to play with. But tonight we had a big leak in the living room ceiling. And I was in such a lousy mood on account of missing the Halloween parade that I made some crack to my mom about our living in a dump. Mom looked really hurt, and then I felt even worse.

My mom is a carpenter. She works very hard. It's

not her fault that Dad left us and we don't have a lot of money. Don't you hate it when you say something that makes someone feel bad and it's too late to take it back?

So I was still feeling pretty low on the subway that night, when we were all riding the A train out of Brooklyn with Mr. Cepeda. The subway car smelled really bad, and the lights kept going on and off. What would we do if the train's power went off and stayed off? We were traveling through a deep underground tunnel. We'd probably be stuck down here for a year—and miss another Halloween.

Gaby reached over and swatted my shoulder. "Will you stop looking so miserable?" she told me.

"This is really what I want to be doing right now," I said, making it very clear that I meant the opposite.

After I had told Alex I had to bag the parade, he had asked Lenni to go with him instead. Lenni had asked Tina, and Tina had asked Jamal. So now the whole rest of the Ghostwriter Team was going to the parade. In fact, Tina was wearing *my* costume. I didn't even know what costumes the rest of them were wearing.

I lowered my voice. "I mean, it's just so unfair," I told Gaby. "The whole rest of the team gets to dress up and we have to . . ."

I waved my hand around at the rest of the class. Besides me and Gaby and Casey, there were only six other kids who had signed up for the trip.

"Oh come on," Casey told me. "Costumes are F.L.K. and so is T. or T."

"Huh?" I said.

"Costumes are F.L.K. and so is T. or T.," she repeated.

"I heard what you said," I told her. "I meant 'Huh?' as in 'What's that supposed to mean?' "

Casey was grinning ear to ear. "It's a kind of riddle," she said. "You have to figure it out."

I groaned. When Casey gets going on her riddles, she can bug you and bug you until you think you're going to lose your marbles. And we had the whole night ahead of us.

"F.L.K.," said Gaby thoughtfully. "From Linda's Kitchen?"

Casey shook her head.

"First Laughing Kangaroo? Fred Leaves Kindergarten?"

Gaby loves this stuff. She'll play a game like this for hours just trying to be the first one to crack the code.

There was an old, homeless guy panhandling for money in our subway car. Mr. Cepeda and I had given him some change. Now the old man was listening to our conversation. "Frank Loves Karen?" he guessed.

"Good guess," Casey told him. "But *wrong!* You guys are all forgetting about a big clue I gave you. You have to think about *everything* I said. Costumes are F.L.K. You have to try to fit the words into the sentence. Costumes are For—"

"Little Kids?" I said, almost without thinking.

Casey bounced up and down in her seat, clapping really hard, so that everyone in the car started staring at us. As annoyed as I was feeling, I still gave a little smile. I had guessed.

"And so is T. or T.," Casey said, reminding us of the rest of the riddle.

"Trick-or-Treating!" Gaby said.

"I shoulda guessed that," the old man said, moving off down the car in search of more change.

It was a chilly night, even in the subway. I thought about giving the old guy my sleeping bag. But for one thing, it didn't belong to me. And for another, Mr. Cepeda had said we'd be sleeping on the floor that night. So I'd really be needing it. On the other hand, I hated to think of that old man being cold. I don't know about you, but I have a whole lot of respect for old people. It's because of my grandfather, *mi abuelo*—he took care of me in Puerto Rico.

But that's another story.

"Okay," Mr. Cepeda was calling, "this is our stop!"

"W.H.," Casey said.

"Don't start," I warned her.

"White House," guessed Gaby.

"We're Here," Casey explained.

I sighed as the train pulled into the station. We

followed Mr. Cepeda out through the turnstiles, past the token booth where the worker was sleeping with her head in her hands, and up a long flight of stairs. When we came out onto the street, the first thing we saw was a newsstand with candy and souvenirs.

So right away we all started begging Mr. Cepeda to let us buy stuff. He was a little annoyed, and he pointed out that we hadn't even gotten to the museum yet. But by then we were all buying soda and candy and gum, so it was too late to stop us.

I got a candy bar called a Museum Munch Bar. I undid the wrapper carefully so it wouldn't rip and put it in my backpack to bring home and add to my collection. The candy was this dark Tootsie Roll kind of stuff, with a different letter stamped on each chocolate section, spelling out MUNCH BAR. It tasted scrumptious, just like the wrapper said it would. I ate right down to the *C*.

The train had let us out on Central Park West. Except for the guy in the newsstand, the street was totally deserted. It was as if we had landed on the moon. And as I stood there eating my candy bar in the cold, my mood started to change. This night was starting to feel like an adventure after all.

Speaking of the moon, it was full. The big white face was staring down at us and making everything look eerie and silver. On one side of the street was Central Park. The trees were all dark and huddled together and scary-looking. It looked as if the trees would try to mug us if we went over there.

On the other side of the street—I had to admit it—the museum looked awesome. It's this huge stone building with big marble pillars. There's an endless flight of stone stairs leading up to the front doors. Hanging down from the roof was a gigantic banner. GO FOR THE GOLD! the banner said, and there was a picture of ten little ancient-looking gold statues.

When Mr. Cepeda gave his talk in assembly, he didn't say anything about gold statues. I might have thought about signing up if I had known. I *wouldn't* have signed up, of course, but I might have *thought* about it.

Right in front of the building, on a huge pedestal, was a statue of some guy on a galloping horse.

"That's T.R.," Gaby said.

"Don't tell me now *you're* starting," I said.

Gaby laughed. "No, that's what people called Teddy Roosevelt. T.R."

"See?" Casey said. "I'm not the only one who likes to play that game."

"Well, who's Teddy Roosevelt?" I asked. I knew Gaby would know. When she's bored, she likes to read the encyclopedia.

The class had gathered around us and Mr. Cepeda nodded at Gaby, so she explained.

"Teddy Roosevelt was the twenty-sixth president of the United States. He was also this really wild character who liked to do daring things, like hunt wild rhinos in Africa or go exploring in the Amazon jungle where there were deadly snakes. When he was just a kid, he started a collection of bones and specimens, and he kept adding to it all his life until it got big enough to start a museum."

My mouth dropped open. I thought about my collection of candy bar wrappers. Wrapper number thirty-one—the Museum Munch Bar—was in my backpack right now. Maybe if I kept adding and adding to the collection, someday they'd start Hector Carrero's Museum of Candy Wrappers. And out front there'd be a statue of me, riding a horse and eating candy.

It was a little before eleven-thirty when Mr. Cepeda led us up the steps to the museum's revolving doors, which were locked and dark. Then a face appeared behind the glass. It belonged to a young security guard who was dressed in a blue uniform like a policeman. He waved us over to a side door. He took out a huge metal ring of keys and started unlocking all sorts of locks and pushing various buttons. Finally he let us in.

"Sorry about that," the guard said. "But we've got a pretty fancy burglar alarm here. Hold on, everybody. I've just got to get this alarm reset."

I watched closely while he locked everything,

pushing lots of buttons on a digital panel. And I thought we had a lot of locks on our apartment door! This museum was as secure as a bank vault.

"Okay," the guard said, "we're all set."

The guard was a tall, muscular guy with a trim black mustache. I noticed he had a big number sewn onto his uniform—4—right above his badge. He shook hands with Mr. Cepeda and handed him a large tag that said GUIDE to wear around his neck.

"How come the lights are off?" asked a kid named Carlos.

"Is everything locked?" asked Alicia Perez.

"Can we go in the gift shop?"

"Where are the bathrooms?"

Everyone was asking questions at once. Mr. Cepeda held up his hands in the dark. "One at a time," he said.

When Mr. Cepeda got us quiet, the guard told us the rules. No touching the exhibits. No shouting. No running in the halls. It sounded like school all over again. Also, we weren't allowed to go anywhere in the museum that wasn't open to the public, like the Herpetology Department, whatever that was. But the guard said all the main exhibits were open for us to see.

"We've even got the Moviemax open," he said.

"What's Moviemax?" asked a kid named Patrick.

The guard explained that Moviemax was a giant movie theater with a screen four stories high.

Excellent, I thought.

"See?" Casey told me. "T.B.C. This Beats Candy."

"And," the guard said with a smile, "you may also go into the newest exhibit—the Great Pyramid of Hoza. It's in the Tomb Room."

A pyramid! *Extra* excellent, I thought.

Just then Gaby tapped me on the back and nodded for me to look up. I nearly fainted dead away. There was a gigantic dinosaur skeleton looming over my head.

"It's a *barosaurus,*" Gaby explained happily.

"Terrific," I said. "What are you trying to do? Give me a heart attack?"

Now that my eyes were adjusting to the dark, I looked around the lobby. From what I could see, the room was big with really high ceilings, like a church. It was the kind of place that looked like it might have vampire bats flying around in it. Right in the middle of the room was the huge dinosaur skeleton that Gaby had pointed out. The long-necked creature was trying to protect its baby from a smaller, ferocious dinosaur skeleton.

These days I've been thinking about being a detective or a spy when I grow up. So I felt pretty foolish for missing three entire dinosaurs. On the other hand, the lobby *was* very dark. And the bones of the skeletons were almost black. I was starting to wonder why we hadn't been told to bring flashlights.

The guard checked his watch and said, "Well, I have to stick to my schedule. Have fun."

And then he was gone.

A dark museum all to ourselves . . . I was ready to go off by myself and investigate.

"Listen up," Mr. Cepeda said. "One more rule. We all have to stick close together."

So much for that.

"But if anyone does get lost"—Mr. Cepeda checked his watch—"we'll meet at the Minerals and Gems exhibit at twelve-thirty sharp. There are maps on the walls that can help you find it."

Mr. C. told us to pile up our sleeping bags on the lobby floor. Then he started down one of the wide halls leading deep into the museum. "C'mon," he called back. "Let's go. Stick close to me."

We all tromped after him.

So there were nine kids filing through a big, dark, empty museum.

Nine kids with backpacks and candy bars and soda pop bottles and mouths full of chewing gum.

Nine kids headed for their doom.

c h a p t e r
two

I consider myself to be pretty brave. For one thing, I live in the projects, like I said. There have been a lot of stray shootings right around there. The fear is something you have to live with.

So I would have thought I could handle walking around a museum after hours no problem.

I was wrong.

I don't know if you've ever been to the Natural History Museum of New York. It's got all these huge dioramas. Sort of like what they make you do in school sometimes, where you build a scene in a shoe box using pipe cleaners and other stuff. Only, at the museum, the exhibits are all life-size, and every detail is made to look perfect.

A lot of the scenes are from ancient life. They have mannequins dressed like Aztecs and other peoples from long ago. Each diorama has a painted backdrop and fake trees and other stuff to make it look really real.

And let me tell you something, you haven't seen these exhibits until you've seen them at night. For one thing, it was dark. The only lights in the whole museum were the lights inside the exhibits, which the museum left on for us like night-lights. Everywhere you looked there were dark shadows, dark shapes, dark corners—places where monsters could hide. In some of the passageways there was so little light we had to hold on to each other and grope our way through.

And then you'd turn the corner and up ahead, looming in the darkness—*Bam!*—you'd suddenly see bright sky and mountains and sunshine and clouds, all behind glass. It was as if we were traveling through time and entering different worlds.

We saw buffalo grazing the Great Plains, zebra trotting up to a water hole in Kenya, and a king cobra raising its hooded head, ready to strike. I got the feeling that if we hung out at the exhibit long enough, the cobra *would* strike. I'm telling you, it was spooky.

Meanwhile, Mr. Cepeda was telling us all kinds of interesting facts about what we were seeing. Like how, up until a hundred years ago, there used to be lots of jaguars roaming around the United States Imagine—jaguars running around Fort Greene!

Then I looked at the jaguars' sharp teeth and hoped they didn't come back—at least not tonight.

Mr. Cepeda showed us a woman from India, dressed as a bride in a headdress made out of gold. She was wearing a veil, so all you could see were her beautiful brown eyes. She was covered with jewelry. I counted nine bracelets on one arm alone—eight gold, one silver. Mr. Cepeda said that the woman and her husband were getting married and were circling the sacred fire seven times.

Somebody getting married . . . there shouldn't have been anything scary about that. But the woman didn't look happy or excited; she looked *mad*. And I just happened to be standing right where she was staring. I couldn't take my eyes off her. And she couldn't take her eyes off me. I shivered.

Mr. Cepeda stopped in front of an exhibit of leopards from Asia. "Listen," he said, lowering his voice. "There's something I forgot to tell you."

Already I was scared, just from his tone of voice.

"I forgot to tell you about a really weird and scary legend."

Oh, great. A weird and scary legend! That was all I needed.

"According to the legend, life is very hard for the creatures and the people in these museum exhibits, because they have to stay so still all year round."

Alicia Perez snorted and said that Mr. Cepeda was

being silly. The mannequins were all made out of wood or metal or something. But Mr. Cepeda didn't look like he was kidding.

"On Halloween night," he went on, "at the stroke of midnight, the exhibits all come to life. They stretch and roam around." He smiled. "Do I need to remind any of you that tonight is Halloween night?"

I shook my head and felt a chill run down my spine.

"So," Mr. Cepeda said with a little smile, "keep your eyes peeled."

"He's joking, right?" Casey asked me.

"Of course," I told her, trying to act like she was babyish for being worried. But the truth was, that legend freaked me out, because I already thought the exhibits looked alive. Could those stuffed vultures get out and bite my face off? How thick was the glass on these exhibits, anyway?

As we followed Mr. Cepeda to the next exhibit, Casey tugged on my arm. She had a smile on her face. Figures. Casey wasn't scared after all. "It's only O.M.T.M.," she told me in a singsong voice.

"Here we go," I said.

"One More . . . ," Gaby said, trying to decode the riddle.

"The word *one* is right," Casey said, grinning even more widely. "*More* is wrong."

"One Minute," Gaby guessed.

Casey clapped. "Don't forget to try to fit it into the sentence."

"It's only One Minute—" Gaby said.

"To Midnight," I said, guessing the rest.

"Yes!" Casey squealed. But then she held her glow-in-the-dark watch up close to her eyes and peered at it. "But," she said, "since it took you so long to guess, it's already *after* midnight."

After midnight.

That meant—

If the legend was true, everything in the museum was coming to life.

chapter
three

Mr. Cepeda stopped in front of an exhibit where some cavemen were making a fire, carving weapons, and preparing dinner. "Now who can tell me how long ago the caveman lived?" he asked.

Hands shot up. Someone guessed a hundred years ago, and then the other kids groaned about how stupid that answer was.

"Actually," Mr. Cepeda said, "they go back a lot further than that. For instance, scientists think that cavemen first came to North America about forty thousand years ago."

I was staring through the glass at the frozen, hairy people sitting around inside. They had low foreheads and big ugly ridges around their eyebrows. They looked a little like apes, which Mr. Cepeda said we're all related to.

They were terrifying-looking, if you want to know

the truth, because their faces and bodies were kind of human and kind of animal.

Then I started thinking . . . what if *these* creatures came to life? We were all alone in the museum. Who would protect us?

It's just a legend, I told myself.

It's just made up.

The class was moving on. I no longer wanted to get separated from the group. Not at all. I wanted lots of people right around me.

"C'mon, Hector," Gaby hissed from down the hall. She and Casey were walking backward behind the group, waving for me to follow.

I was about to. But I couldn't help turning around and taking one last peek at the exhibit.

In the dark shadows in the back of the exhibit, there was a bearded caveman sitting frozen in the act of sharpening a wooden ax.

His head was down, so I couldn't see his face very well.

Then he slowly lifted his head and stared right at me.

The caveman's eyes were dark, ancient. He looked as if he recognized me—even though he came from thousands of years ago.

I tottered backward. My jaw dropped. I was too scared to speak. But somehow I started screaming. The sound just poured out of me.

The whole class came pounding back down the hallway.

"Wh-What?" Mr. Cepeda demanded, out of breath. "What's wrong?"

I pointed. "There. The caveman."

But the caveman had his head down again, in the same position it was in before.

"What about him?" Mr. Cepeda growled.

"He's alive!" I said.

The whole class pressed right up against the glass,

yelling, "Which one?" and knocking on the glass, as if to get the cavemen's attention.

"It's the one way in the back," I said. "He was looking right at me."

I was starting to feel very foolish. Had I really seen the caveman move? I was sure I had . . . wasn't I?

"He's staying still because you're all here," I said, feeling my face get all red. "A minute ago, he picked his head right up and stared at me. I swear."

"Right," Carlos said. "And the caveman by the fire sang you 'Happy Birthday.' "

"It happened!" I said.

Mr. Cepeda was giving me a disappointed look that made me feel all squirmy inside. "That was a good joke," he said, "but we've got a lot of museum to cover before everyone gets too sleepy. So if you don't mind, Hector, no more practical jokes."

"I wasn't joking," I insisted. But I could see Mr. Cepeda didn't believe me. Even Gaby and Casey were giving me funny looks.

"I swear it's true," I told them. "He picked his head up and stared right at me. It made my blood run cold."

"You're teasing," Casey said happily. I could tell she was glad someone else had gotten in trouble for joking around—for once.

"You believe me, don't you?" I asked Gaby.

"Well, I believe you *think* it happened," Gaby said

thoughtfully. She put an arm around my shoulder, which made me feel like I was about two years old. "All that talk about the legend probably got your mind going. You've got such a great imagination. Probably your eyes played a trick on you."

"Let's go, guys," Mr. Cepeda called, starting down the hall. We hurried to catch up.

Mr. Cepeda showed us an African giant called Ndzingi. Ndzingi had this huge—and I mean *huge*—head made out of twigs and bark cloth. He had a beard of straw and a big red hole for a mouth. Mr. Cepeda said that the Mbwela people in Angola used to believe that Ndzingi could swallow a dog whole.

"Now how's that for a Halloween costume?" Mr. Cepeda asked us, smiling. He told us that the costume was worn by members of the tribe during special ceremonies and was supposed to inspire fear.

It was working.

As a matter of fact, I was having a really hard time keeping my mind on what Mr. Cepeda was saying. First I kept picturing that big red mouth of Ndzingi swallowing *me* whole. Then I kept picturing that caveman's dark eyes, boring into mine. He did look at me. He did!

Our tour continued, but I couldn't calm down. Every time I tried to study an exhibit, I felt like the exhibit was studying *me*. The dark eyes of a giant squid—weren't they staring right at me? I also kept hearing strange noises. Weren't those big hairy buffaloes stamping their hooves?

It takes a lot for Mr. Cepeda to lose his temper. But I could tell he was starting to get mad at me. And that was before I told the class that I saw the elephant breathing.

"Hector," Mr. Cepeda said. He said my name pretty sharply, like he was really going to let me have it. But then he took a deep breath and went back to his usual soft patient voice. "Listen, Hector, it's enough with that joke already."

"It's not a joke, I'm telling you—"

"Look! I only told you about that legend to get you all to pay more attention, not so you would goof off."

"So you made up the legend?" I asked, feeling incredibly relieved.

"No, I didn't make it up," Mr. Cepeda said. "But a legend is just a story that got passed around. It's not true. Now come on!"

As Mr. C. continued his tour, I could see Gaby and Casey giving me angry looks in the dark.

"*What*?" I said, feeling hurt.

"I know what you're doing," Gaby said.

"What are you talking about? I'm not doing anything."

"You're just trying to get us back for signing you up for the trip. You're trying to scare us."

"Yeah," Casey agreed, "only it's not working. So you can just D.I., Drop It."

"Gaby, Casey," I said, feeling really frustrated now, "I promise you, I'm not trying to scare you. I'm telling the truth."

I saw the look Casey was giving me. She shook her head slowly. I sighed. "I wish the rest of the team were here," I muttered. "They'd believe me, I know it."

"They wouldn't," Casey said. The way she said it—so confidently—kind of ticked me off. She's the newest team member, after me. How could she know what the rest of the team would think without even asking them?

Then I had an idea. "Okay, okay, okay. Time out," I told them. "You don't believe me, right?"

Their expressions told me their answer.

"So how about giving me a chance to prove it to you? C'mon, *one* chance!"

They both looked very doubtful.

The class was moving on to the next exhibit. "Stay back one second," I told Gaby and Casey in a low voice. "And I'll show you what I'm talking about. I've got an idea for how we can catch these exhibits moving."

"Hector," Gaby said wearily, sounding like my mom when she gets fed up with me.

"Just do this one thing," I said, "and then I promise I won't bring it up again. That is—if I'm wrong."

I could hear Mr. Cepeda at the next exhibit, talking about how you could make arrowheads by banging two stones together. "Here's what we do," I whispered to Gaby and Casey. We huddled together while I told them my plan.

We were standing in front of an exhibit that showed a cutaway model of an American Indian longhouse. It was a big wood and bark building where several Iroquois were grinding corn in wooden bowls. The mannequins weren't moving, of course. We looked into the glass for a few seconds more, then casually started strolling away. Casey even whistled.

Then we ducked down and crawled back, keeping below the glass front of the exhibit so we were hidden from the mannequins inside.

"This is ridiculous," Gaby whispered.

"Shh!" I said.

But Casey started giggling. Which probably tipped off the mannequins that we were coming. Because when we popped up into view, the mannequins weren't moving.

"Satisfied?" Gaby asked me.

I wasn't. I stared hard at one of the Iroquois figures, trying to catch it moving.

"Hector," Casey said, tugging on my arm, "you said if we did this one trick you would drop the whole thing."

Casey always remembers exactly what you say,

word for word, which can be very annoying when you try to change your mind about something. I shrugged my arm free.

I was studying one of the Iroquois figures from the tips of his head-feathers down to the shoelaces of his moccasins, but it remained perfectly still, as still as a statue.

And then I heard Casey say, "Uh-oh."

I looked up.

Casey was staring down the dark, wide hallway.

"Uh-oh what?" I asked.

Casey didn't answer. But Gaby, who was looking down the hallway, said, "Oh no."

I stepped back from the exhibit, half expecting to see a wild jaguar charging at us.

Instead what I saw was . . .

Nothing.

The dark hallway was utterly deserted.

Mr. Cepeda and the class were nowhere in sight.

chapter five

"Mr. Cepeda!" Gaby called.

There was no answer. Just this total awful silence. Then we started running.

I was praying that we would see the class as soon as we turned the next corner.

We didn't. We just saw a wide, dark, empty hallway, lit by the exhibits. And those exhibits—I knew without looking—were all slowly coming to life.

We kept running, turning this way and that. But the museum is full of winding, twisty paths leading through the exhibits. First we ended up in front of human skeletons watching TV. The sign over the exhibit said something about evolution. I didn't even know what that was, but I sure wasn't going to stick around to find out.

We kept running and calling for the class, but we

didn't know which way to turn. We were just getting more and more lost. And out of breath.

"H-Hold on," I said, stopping in front of a long dugout canoe full of Chilkat Indians. "This is hopeless," I said. "The museum is too big. We'll never find them."

Casey and Gaby didn't say anything. We all just looked at each other. And from the looks Casey and Gaby were giving me, I knew they were blaming me for getting us lost.

"I know, I know," I said. "It's my fault. But have no fear, Hector Carrero is here. And I have a solution."

I pointed to a map on the wall. "We just have to figure out how to get to the Hall of Minerals and Gems in"—I checked Gaby's watch and gulped—"five minutes."

We ran to the wall map. "Here!" Casey cried, pointing to a picture of a big diamond. "That diamond must stand for the gems."

"We are here," Gaby said, pointing to a red arrow.

I traced our route along the map, and then we started running again. We made it to the Hall of Minerals and Gems in four minutes. So we were right on time to meet up with Mr. Cepeda and the rest of the group.

But the hall was empty.

"They'll be here," I promised, feeling very unsure.

The Hall of Minerals and Gems is a pretty fantastic-looking place. If we hadn't been lost, and if there wasn't a caveman who had just given me the hairy eyeball, I would have enjoyed it. There were all these amazing rocks and diamonds and other jewels floating in beams of light. The rest of the space was pitch dark.

Just then, Gaby gasped.

Which made Casey shriek and made me almost faint. "What is it?" I asked.

" 'The five-hundred-sixty-three-carat Star of India is the biggest star sapphire in the world,' " Gaby said, studying an exhibit. "Look at this thing, it comes all the way from Sri Lanka."

"Yeah," I said, trying to get my heart to slow down, "beautiful."

Casey laughed. Then she started skipping around the room. "Who wants to play hopscotch?" she asked.

I couldn't believe it. She wasn't even slightly scared. Or maybe she was just a great actress and hiding her true feelings.

We didn't play hopscotch. We might as well have. Because we sat around waiting and waiting but Mr. Cepeda and the other kids didn't show. A lot of the time none of us said a word. We were so still and quiet you could hear the hum of the tiny exhibit lights.

Finally I asked, "He did say if we got lost we were supposed to come here, right? I mean, *that* wasn't my mind playing tricks on me, was it?"

After you have an ancient caveman look right at you, you start doubting everything.

"Hey," Gaby said. She slapped her forehead as if she had been really dumb. "I know who can help us find the class . . ."

Casey and I both finished her thought along with her—

"Ghostwriter!"

I still haven't told you about him. He's this ghost who helps me and my teammates solve mysteries. Who is Ghostwriter? That's the biggest mystery of all. We have no idea. We just know he writes to us, and we write back, and he's our friend. He can't see anything except letters, but it still comes in handy having a ghost on your side, let me tell you. Like now, for instance.

Gaby took out her notebook. She took off her pen. On the Ghostwriter Team, you always wear a pen on a string around your neck so you can write to Ghostwriter at any moment.

"GHOSTWRITER," she wrote then, "WE'RE LOST." She paused, looking up at us. "What can I tell him to help him find Mr. Cepeda?"

I tried to picture our teacher and remember if he was wearing anything with writing on it, stuff Ghostwriter could see.

"He's wearing that big guide pass," I said.

"Perfect!" said Gaby. Then she wrote, "PLEASE FIND 'GUIDE.' THEN READ WHAT'S NEAR-BY."

There was a green glow as Ghostwriter read her message. I was awfully glad to see him. I saw Gaby and Casey smile as well, so I knew they felt the same way. With Ghostwriter here to help us, I figured we wouldn't be lost for long.

The letters of Gaby's message spun in the air as Ghostwriter rearranged them. He wrote back, Found Guide, flashing the letters happily.

We cheered.

Then he wrote, H BAR.

We all stared at the message in silence.

"Maybe that's the name of the cafeteria," I suggested.

Casey ran to look at the map, skipping again, as if we weren't in the middle of a crisis. "Nope," she sang out, "the cafeteria is called the Caveman Café." She laughed. "I wonder if they serve cavemen? Get it?"

"We get it, we get it," I said. "So what does 'H Bar' stand for?"

No one had any idea. "PLEASE READ MORE," Gaby wrote.

This time Ghostwriter came back with a long message about arrows and spearpoints.

Now we were getting somewhere. "Arrows!" I

said. "That's right where we were when we got lost!"

I was about to run out, but Gaby grabbed the sleeve of my shirt. "Hold it. Arrows could mean a lot of different American Indian tribes."

"So?" I said.

"So there are loads of American Indian exhibits in the museum. There's the Eastern Woodlands and Plains Indians, and there's the Northwest Coast Indians, there's the . . ."

I was starting to feel less excited.

"Besides," Gaby said, "we don't even know if it's American Indians we're looking for. Cavemen used arrows, too, and so did the ancient Egyptians—"

I stopped listening. The museum was a huge place. With four floors in this building alone, the entire complex took up several city blocks. Right then I started to realize we were going to be all alone all night.

Luckily, before I got more depressed, Ghostwriter started writing us a new message:

The Great Sphin, about 4500 years old, has a human head and the body of a lion.

"Great," I said to Gaby. "Now you're going to tell me that there are all sorts of Great Sphins, whatever they are, right?"

Gaby didn't answer right away. She was studying the message. "A human head and the body of a lion. Hmmm," she said. "I used to know what that was called . . ."

Just my luck. The one time Gaby Fernandez forgets a piece of trivia!

And then we heard footsteps.

Casey ran to the double doors and opened them. "We're in here!" she called.

There was no answer.

For once, Casey didn't look so carefree. And she didn't skip on the way back.

"See?" I asked triumphantly. "You guys heard those footsteps, too, right?"

"Right," Gaby said. "It's probably Mr. Cepeda." But I noticed she was whispering.

We all listened. We heard more footsteps, followed by creaking sounds, rasping sounds, and grating sounds, as if the exhibits were all moving around out there.

"Okay," I said finally. "Maybe we should try to speed it up here. Gaby, have you ever heard of the Great Sphin?"

"Never," Gaby said.

"Terrific. Well, if you haven't heard of it, neither have—"

I stopped talking so suddenly that Casey grabbed my arm. "What is it?" she demanded. I could tell she was finally starting to get as freaked out as I was.

I had just remembered something. Ghostwriter can't write letters on his own. He can only write to us by rearranging the letters he finds nearby. Maybe there was a letter missing from his message because there was a letter we hadn't given him to use. I took Gaby's notebook and flipped through the pages, most of which were blank. With so little writing to choose from, maybe Ghostwriter had needed a letter that Gaby had never used. I started writing out the alphabet.

"Hector," Casey teased, "this isn't the time to practice your writing skills."

"Very funny," I said. But the truth was, I was already starting to doubt my plan. I had written *A* through *P* and no letters had moved. Ghostwriter didn't seem to be interested. *Don't give up,* I told myself. I kept writing. *Q, R, S, T . . .*

"Hector," Gaby said, "you mind telling us what you're doing?"

"Wait," I said. I kept writing. *U, V, W, X.*

The moment I wrote the X it glowed green and began to jiggle up and down as if it were coming to life.

Ghostwriter flew the X down and inserted it into his message. So now the end of the line read The Great Sphinx.

"Which is in Egypt," said our very own walking encyclopedia, Gaby.

"The Hall of Ancient Egypt," I said, standing.

Casey was already running back to the map.

"The entrance to the hall is on the second floor," she called back to us.

I started running for the door. I stopped. Those footsteps. I wasn't hearing them now. But what if that was because all the creatures had already arrived outside the doors? What if the lions were lined up, waiting to pounce? What if those huge Andean condors were silently gliding around, their gigantic wings spread wide? What if—

I yanked open the door fast, like you're supposed to do with a Band-Aid to make the pain go fast. There was no one outside.

"Let's go," I said, sounding a lot braver than I felt.

We ran back through the exhibits to the wide stone staircase that led up to the second floor. We followed the wall maps and the big signs to the Hall of Ancient Egypt, occasionally letting out a shout to tell Mr. Cepeda where we were. We didn't hear a peep out of Mr. Cepeda, but as we got closer to the Hall, we did hear more footsteps. Louder, this time.

We stood stock-still. Then we slowly turned around.

Just in time to see an Iroquois Indian creeping past the next bend in the dark hallway.

My heart stopped. *I'm not seeing this,* I told myself. *It's just my imagination.*

But I could hear the Indian's long leather leggings rustling slightly as he moved. I could see his two black braids swinging. I could see he was bare-chested and strong-looking. And in his hand I could see something glinting—a silver knife!

Then he was gone.

I gulped. Or tried to. I kind of got stuck midgulp. My mouth had gone bone-dry. I found that I was gripping Gaby with one hand and Casey with the other. And they were holding on to me, too. Hard. We were suddenly all glued together.

"You guys saw that too, right?" I asked.

They nodded at me in the darkness.

The whole time since the caveman gave me that look, I'd been hoping that someone else would see the exhibits moving so I wouldn't seem like such a fool. But now that Casey and Gaby had seen a mannequin come to life, I was wishing with all my might that the whole thing had just stayed in my head.

We all started moving as one, backing away from where we saw the Iroquois Indian walk by.

We bumped into something.

We turned around.

There stood the caveman, his ancient stone ax raised high over our heads.

chapter SIX

I ran faster than I've ever run in my life. Seriously, I wish there had been someone around to time me, because I think I might have broken the world's record for the hundred-yard dash, racing down that hallway.

The caveman was right behind us, his bare feet slapping against the stone floor. He was grunting in frustration as he tried to catch us.

It was only as we got to the end of the hallway that I remembered we were headed right toward the Iroquois Indian.

I was running too fast to stop. I only had time to pray that the thing I'd seen glinting in the Indian's hand wasn't really a—

Knife. Yes, it definitely was a knife, because as we reached the end of the hallway the Indian sprang out at us with the knife in his hand.

So now we had two people chasing us. And now we were running even faster, which I wouldn't have thought possible a second before, but as it turned out, it was.

We clattered down the wide, stone steps to the first floor of the museum. I was taking so many steps at a time I was sure I was going to turn into a little ball and roll down. I figured I'd be dead before I hit bottom, which would be a relief in a way because the caveman and the Iroquois Indian were gaining on us.

We started ducking through the winding paths of the museum, trying to take sharp turns left and right, trying to throw them off the track. On the other hand, Gaby and Casey kept screaming, which was telling them exactly where we were.

That wasn't very smart, right? But the thing was, I was doing my share of the screaming, so I couldn't blame them.

Finally we were so out of breath we had to stop. We just stood there, our shoulders heaving, expecting the knife and the ax to slice into us at any instant.

Then Casey pointed at the sign painted on the door behind us.

HERPETOLOGY DEPARTMENT—ONE FLIGHT UP

Gaby pointed to the words painted underneath that.

NOT OPEN TO THE PUBLIC

That didn't stop us for long. So what if we got

arrested? It was better than getting axed! Where was that security guard, anyway? We opened the door and ran up another flight of stairs. We ducked into a dark room.

I mean *dark*. When the door closed behind us, I couldn't even see my own hands. All I could hear was the three of us panting loudly.

"Shh," I forced out.

But there was no way we could stop breathing, unless, of course, the two mannequins caught up with us. When they were done with us, we'd stop breathing for sure.

"Herpetology," Casey said. "I wonder what that means."

I waited for Gaby to give us the answer. Instead, she said, "I don't know, I've never heard that word before."

"Listen," I whispered, "I don't think this is a good time to add to our vocabulary skills, because if we keep making noise, we're going to get our heads chopped off."

"You're the one who's talking," Casey whispered angrily.

"No, you are," I said louder.

"No, you are," she said back.

Very mature, I know, but neither one of us was thinking too clearly.

"Herpetology," Gaby repeated softly. "Well, let's see . . . I know that words that end with *ology* usually mean some kind of science. Like there's *psychology:* that's the science of the mind. So this must be the science of herpet."

"Fascinating," I said, "but don't you think we'd be better off right now if we wrote another message to Ghostwriter and tried to get some help?"

"It's kind of dark," Casey pointed out.

"Well, I'm going to try," I said. I knelt down, wiping away the dust on the floor with the palm of my hand. "And Casey, stop hissing at me."

"I'm not hissing at you."

"Yes you are."

"No I'm not."

"Guys," Gaby said, "do you know how silly you sound?"

I didn't answer. I was too busy trying to write straight in the pitch darkness. "DEAR ALEX, TINA, LENNI, JAMAL," I wrote. "WE NEED YOUR HELP REAL BAD. WE'RE IN THE MUSEUM AND THE EXHIBITS ARE COMING TO LIFE! RIGHT NOW WE'RE STUCK IN A STRANGE DARK ROOM. PLEASE CALL THE POLICE!—H"

Here came the familiar green glow, carrying the letters to the rest of the team.

Usually I find that green glow very comforting, because it means that Ghostwriter is around. But this time, the glow provided just enough light for me to see what was in the room.

"Now I know what *herpetology* means," Casey said, wide-eyed.

The room was filled with snakes! I only caught a brief glimpse, like I said. But I could see the snakes were all wriggling and slithering and some of them were raising their heads.

Then the green glow was gone and we were back in the dark, but now we were standing stock-still and listening. We could hear the sound of dry skin rubbing against itself as the snakes slid around in their cages.

I let out a low moan. It felt like my insides were falling out, I was so scared. I was too scared to run. But I was between Casey and Gaby and the door, so when they started to run, they crashed into me. And that got me going.

Except I guess I didn't run straight at the door. Because the next thing I knew we smashed into a wall of glass cages. I could feel the cages rock backward—about to go over—carrying us along with them. I reached out my hand and grabbed on to something, trying to steady myself.

The cages didn't go over. I righted myself, but I must have grabbed on to the door to the one of the cages, because I could feel it swing open in my hand. And then I heard the loudest rattling hiss I'd ever heard in my life. Then we were running again, and this time we found the door.

Great, I thought as we raced down the steps. *Now we've got snakes after us too.*

We didn't stop running until we got to the bottom of the stairwell. We looked back up. There weren't any snakes slithering down toward us, at least not that I could see.

"I thought the museum was only for dead things," Casey said.

"No," said Gaby. "The museum has different departments that study live things, too."

"Great," said Casey.

"Hey," I said. I'd just had another terrifying thought. "Maybe those snakes used to be dead," I pointed out. "And now they're coming to life just like . . ."

We all listened for a second. I was expecting to hear the distant trumpeting of giant elephants.

"C'mon!" I cried. I grabbed Casey's and Gaby's hands, giving a tug to make sure they followed me as I started to run. I sure didn't want to go anywhere by myself at the moment.

I was in the lead. I wasn't sure where I was running to, but as I ran, a sort of plan formed in my head:

Get out of this museum!

I started following the red Exit signs, hoping they would lead us out onto the street where we could scream for the police.

We almost made it back to the lobby where we came in, but just then—

A huge figure jumped out at us.

It was the African giant, Ndzingi! The one with the huge round head and the big red mouth that could swallow dogs whole!

Now I had a new plan:

Run the other way!

This time I led Gaby and Casey to the stairs to the second floor. I made it to the first landing and was turning the corner when I saw her.

The mannequin dressed as a bride from India was standing at the top of the stairs. Her tall gold headdress shone in the dim light. She smiled. Then she beckoned us to come closer, slowly waving her hand. When she moved, her jewelry made sweet tinkly sounds, like wind chimes. And her nine bracelets slid up and down her wrist.

I wasn't tempted to go chat with her, believe me. Somehow I didn't think that the bride was planning to invite us to her wedding party.

We ran back down the steps the other way. I didn't look back, but I could tell by the loud rustling of skirts and clanking of jewelry that the Indian bride was rushing down the stairs after us.

Casey was ahead now. She led us through the exhibits of Northwest Coast Indians. We were running fast, which was good, because it meant I didn't have time to look at all the exhibits on either side of us. We were surrounded by mannequins. Mannequins who were looking out at us. Mannequins who would be coming to life soon and joining the chase.

Casey led us to the exhibit marked North American Mammals. In the back of my head, I was trying to think what we had seen there. Then I remembered—the buffalo!

Casey had her hands on the doors when we heard footsteps thundering toward us on the other side.

My blood turned to ice. "The buffalo!" I gasped. "They're stampeding toward us!"

I turned. Behind us, we could hear more footsteps approaching. There were figures coming for us from that way.

We were caught.

The only thing that saved us was that Gaby got so scared, she just fell backward. She was leaning up against this big set of double doors. As she fell, the doors swung open and she landed inside.

We raced after her. The doors closed and again we were hiding in the dark.

Out in the hall we could hear the footsteps coming closer . . .

And closer . . .

And then the footsteps passed by.

We were safe.

We all gave one big sigh.

Then we turned around.

Just as the giant *Tyrannosaurus rex* swooped its massive head down, its jaws opened wide to tear us into tiny pieces.

chapter
seven

I ducked back so hard I smacked my head against the door.

But I didn't duck back far enough. The dinosaur closed its massive jaws around my body and munched me into bloody mincemeat. Then it lifted its head high in the air, chewing happily with a terrible evil glint in its little dinosaur eyes.

"It's—a—movie!" Gaby said, choking out the words. "It's a movie."

I looked down. I was still standing right where I'd been standing a split-second before and I was still whole. The body that the dinosaur was chewing up on the screen wasn't mine.

A movie! We all started jumping up and down and holding each other and saying it over and over again. Movie, movie, movie! The dinosaur wasn't real. We weren't dino-dinner. We were still alive.

"C'mon," Gaby said. She led the way into one of the rows of plush seats. We all crouched down. Up on the huge screen, there were more life-size dinosaurs attacking. It was hard not to look. It was also hard not to duck.

Gaby was writing in her notebook. "Alex, Lenni, Jamal, and Tina," she whispered as she wrote. "We're in big trouble. We need your help. Like Hector told you, the museum exhibits are all coming to life! Please call the police and please come right away!"

Then we waited.

And waited. But even though Ghostwriter quickly flew off with the letters, there was no response.

"Please answer," I said aloud. My voice shook a little when I said it. And I noticed that my body was trembling all over, like the hummingbird Mr. Cepeda let us hold on our last field trip, which was to the Bronx Zoo.

I looked over at Casey to see if she had noticed how scared I was and was going to tease me. A big tear was slowly inching down her cheek. So she *was* scared, after all. I reached out my hand. She grabbed it and held on.

"They're probably so distracted with the parade and everything they keep missing Ghostwriter's message," Gaby said softly, studying her notebook.

Casey and I didn't answer. It had been terrifying getting chased through the hall by a caveman with an ax. But in a way, waiting was worse. It was as if we were tied down to train tracks, waiting for a train to hit us. We couldn't move. And it was up to our friends to come and untie us.

"I'm S.O.O.M.M.," I told Casey.

She decoded it fast.

"Scared Out Of My Mind."

We didn't smile at each other, but still, the joke helped calm us down a little bit.

"There!" Casey cried as Ghostwriter's green glow zoomed around the notebook.

We all read the message together. **The exhibits are coming to life? Nice try. Happy Halloween to you, too. Alex.**

I groaned and smacked my forehead. "They don't believe us."

"Try it again," Casey urged Gaby.

"No," Gaby said, "we'll never convince them. I wouldn't believe it if I hadn't seen it for myself."

"So now what?" I asked.

"Maybe we can hide here until tomorrow morning," Gaby suggested.

"No way," Casey said. "It's too awful just waiting around."

"Casey's right," I agreed. "And sooner or later those creatures will find us."

"What do they want with us?" Casey wondered.

"I don't know," Gaby shrugged. "To kill us, I guess."

"But why?" Casey asked.

It was a good question. I had no idea. I hoped we never found out.

"Look," I said, "Our only hope is to try to make it back to Mr. Cepeda. I mean, there's safety in numbers, right?"

Gaby and Casey looked doubtful.

"Okay," Gaby said, "so I guess that means we have to try to make it back to the Hall of Ancient Egypt."

"Without ending up like those skeletons in the Evolution exhibit," I said. I wasn't laughing.

We had decided to leave, but nobody moved.

"Look!" Casey pointed at the gigantic screen. The dinosaurs were still lunging at us. But Ghostwriter had carried some of our letters up there to make a huge message on top of the dinosaurs:

Hang in there. I'll keep trying to get help.

"Thanks, Ghostwriter," Casey said aloud. And then the dinosaurs seemed to chew up the message as the letters disappeared.

"Okay," I said. "Let's go."

We came out of our hiding place and started tiptoeing toward the door.

We made it out into the hallway with no problem. Around the first bend, no problem. But that wasn't too reassuring, because we knew that a very *big* problem could leap out at us at any moment.

My heart was pounding. It was so loud in my chest, it sounded as if the mannequins in one of the African exhibits had come to life and were pounding away on their gourd skins. Which they probably were.

Every time we came to the end of a hallway, we'd peek around the corner before going any farther. We were looking behind us all the time. So it was pretty slow going. But we made it up to the second floor without running into any more monsters.

We were tiptoeing down the hall toward the Tomb Room when Casey stopped short. "What's this?" she asked, picking up a folded piece of white paper that had been lying on the floor.

"Leave it!" I whispered.

But Casey was unfolding it.

"Casey!" I said, a little louder, squeezing her arm.

"It looks like some kind of schedule," she said, ignoring me.

Gaby was looking over Casey's shoulder, so I looked too. The note was handwritten in pencil:

H.O.A.E.

G.S.

#1
11:45 - 12:30 T.R.
12:30 - 1:00 1st floor
1:00 - 1:45 3rd floor
1:45 - 2:15 T.R.

#2
11:45 - 12:15 T.R.
12:15 - 12:45 4th floor
12:45 - 1:15 T.R.
1:15 - 2:00 T.R.

#3
11:45 - 12:15 1st floor
12:15 - 12:45 T.R.

#3
12:45 - 1:15 2nd floor
1:15 - 1:45 T.R.

#4
11:30 - 12:30 3rd floor
12:30 - 1:00 T.R.
1:00 - 1:30 1st floor
1:30 - 2:00 4th floor

#5
11:45 - 12:15 4th floor
12:15 - 12:45 3rd floor
12:45 - 1:15 2nd floor
1:15 - 2:15 T.R.

"Weird," Casey said. "I wonder what it is."

"It's something we don't have time for, that's what it is," I said, trying to look as stern as possible.

"Hector's right," Gaby told her, tugging on her arm. "Come on."

But Casey kept looking at the note as we crept down the hallway.

It was only when we heard the man singing that Casey looked up.

The voice was coming from up ahead, in the Tomb Room.

We all froze. I could see terror in Casey's and Gaby's faces, and I'm sure mine looked the same.

Then I realized something. I recognized what the person was singing. I happen to be into popular music. The song was "Dead Souls" by a group called Nine Inch Nails. A real comforting choice of music, by the way.

Gaby's face relaxed a little. "That's no caveman," she whispered.

"How do you know?" I whispered back.

"Because how would a caveman know that song?" Casey asked.

"Right," said Gaby.

"Yeah," I whispered, "but they've been sitting in those exhibits all year. Every day they hear people outside with their radios and Walkmans. Maybe he learned the tune."

"There's your wild imagination again," Gaby said, shaking her head.

"Was it my imagination when the American Indian attacked us with a knife? Was it my imagination when that bride chased us down the stairs? Was it my imagination when—"

"Okay, okay, you've got a point," Gaby agreed.

So we stole into the Tomb Room as cautiously as we could.

Up ahead, in the darkness, loomed an enormous pointy shape. It was the Great Pyramid of Hoza the

guard told us about! We looked around. We didn't see anyone. And the singing had stopped.

Suddenly a hand clapped down on my back and a voice boomed, "Hold it right there!"

I must have jumped about twenty feet in the air, and I'm not exaggerating. Seriously, if this had been jump ball in a basketball game and I was up against Shaquille O'Neal, right then I would have beat him out for the ball.

Then we heard chuckling. It was security guard number 4, the tall muscular guy with the mustache who had let us into the building in the first place.

Guard number 4 was still laughing. "What do you kids think you're doing, sneaking around like that? Why aren't you with your class?"

Now that I was over my initial horror and my heart had started back up again, I was delighted to see the guard. In fact, I wanted to fall at his feet and hug his legs. But for a second, I couldn't speak, and neither could Gaby or Casey. And then, when we did start speaking, we all started speaking at once. So it came out sort of like this:

"All - This - An - the - caveman - American Indian - museum-is-is-exhibits-chasing-after-are-us-us-coming-with-with-to-an-a-life!-ax!-knife!"

If you read every third word starting with the first word, you can figure out what I said. And if you read every third word starting with the second word, you can figure out what Gaby said. And if you read every third word starting with the third word, you can figure out what Casey said. But the guard just heard us all talking at once. He shook his head and said, "Come again?"

So we said:

"This-An-I-dinosaur-Indian-think-attacked-bride -the-us-was-rattlesnakes-but-waving-got-that-to- loose-was-us-and-just-from-are-a-the-after-movie!- stairs!-us!"

The guard grabbed me and shook me. "Hold it!" he said. "Slow down. Quiet, all of you! Now, one at a time." He looked at me. "You first."

So in between gulping for air I started telling him. But I didn't make a lot more sense than I had when we were all talking at once. I was close to tears, and out of breath, and my words were tumbling out of me like they were falling down a long flight of stairs.

"Let me tell," Casey said. She gave the guard her best smile and said very clearly, "The exhibits are all coming to life."

The guard's eyebrows shot up. And then he threw back his head and roared with laughter.

I grabbed his arm. "Quiet! They'll hear you."

That only made him laugh harder. "Who'll hear me? The buffalo?"

"Yes!"

"That's a good one, kids," he said, wiping his eyes. "You're trying to give me a happy Halloween, aren't ya?"

We all looked at each other. The guard had come to the same conclusion as Alex and our other Ghostwriter teammates.

"Everything okay?" a deep voice called.

For the first time, I noticed there was another guard on the other side of the pyramid, hidden in the shadows. I couldn't see him too well, but I could see that this was one was bald.

"All okay," said guard number 4. "Just some of our young campers playing a little gag."

The other guard waved and stepped back into the darkness.

We must have all gotten the same idea at once, because right then we all started tugging on the guard's arms, trying to pull him back toward the door.

"We'll show you," I said.

"Whoa," he said. "Not so fast. I can't leave my post. I'm on a strict schedule. But I'm off in—let's see." He checked his watch. "It's twelve forty-seven now. I'm off in thirteen minutes. I promise you I'll take a look around then. And if I see any elephants roaming around, you can be sure I'll arrest them. Ha-ha."

"But you've got to believe us," Casey said. "I mean, do you think all three of us would make up a story like that?"

The guard wasn't paying any attention to her. Apparently he did believe all three of us would make up a story like that. He had taken his walkie-talkie off his belt. "I'm going to get you hooked back up with the rest of your group," he explained.

There was a buzz of static and garbled voices as he contacted the other night guards. But none had seen Mr. Cepeda and the rest of the class. "Don't worry," guard number 4 told us. "There are five of us on duty here at night. We'll find them."

He smiled. "In the meantime, let me show you kids the pyramid. It's the coolest exhibit the museum's had in a while."

An hour ago, I would have been excited to see the pyramid. But right now, all I wanted to see was the outside of the museum. "Please," I begged, "you've got to believe us, the exhibits are coming to—"

"Now, now," he said harshly, "enough of that. You tried your joke and you had your fun; enough's enough."

He was pushing us over to the pyramid. He was strong, too.

"Now I'm no tour guide," the guard said, "but believe me, I've heard their spiel often enough to give it to you. This is the Tomb of Hoza."

"Mister," Gaby began, her eyes flashing with anger, "we're all going to get eaten up in a few minutes by—"

"Now, I should tell you, everything you saw in the museum tonight was real."

He got that right.

"What I mean is, you saw models of things that actually existed once. But this pyramid is an exception. There was never a real Great Pyramid of Hoza. The museum made it up to give you kids a fun time. This is one of the few exhibits in the museum that you can touch. And the pyramid teaches you some stuff about the real pyramids."

I was keeping my eyes on the entrance to the Tomb Room. I was expecting to see that caveman burst through those doors any second. He didn't. In the meantime, the guard was pushing us into a small, dark gap in the pyramid's stone wall—an entrance.

"Sir?" Gaby said. "Could I use your walkie-talkie for a second? We have a friend on the police force. A Lieutenant McQuade? He'll be very interested to hear what we have to tell him, believe me. And if you help us, there might even be a reward for—hey!"

The guard lifted Gaby up off the ground to get her through the pyramid doorway. "One more thing," the guard said. "The exhibit isn't real, but the treasure inside *is*. They're showing off ten little gold statues. They say they're worth millions. But don't even *think* about trying to steal one."

"We wouldn't," I started, "we just want to get out of the museum alive and—"

"Because," the guard said, "this exhibit is absolutely thief-proof. Mr. Bell, the director of the museum, personally oversaw the security plans for this baby." The guard slapped the side of the pyramid. It sounded solid.

"Yup. During the day, there are all these people going in and out of the museum, right? But they have five—count 'em, five—security guards stationed in the Tomb Room all day to make sure no one walks off with anything. And at night? Forget about it. We have another five guards on duty all night and two of them are always in the Tomb Room. And there are so many burglar alarms set up at every entrance to the museum, there's no way a burglar could get in or out of the building."

He had pushed us all inside. He smiled. "Go ahead. Check it out. You'll love it."

We didn't have much choice. We turned and started walking single-file down a long narrow passageway, farther into the pyramid.

"Don't worry, guys. This is probably as good a place to hide as any," Gaby said, up ahead.

"Yeah," Casey said in a hushed voice. "Who would think to look for us in here?"

Which was when the loud voice boomed right in my ear.

chapter
eight

"Welcome to the museum's Great Pyramid of Hoza!" blasted the voice. "Or should we say, tomb robbers, beware!"

I shrank back, ready to run. Then I realized it was a tape-recorded voice, part of the exhibit.

The announcer went on, "In ancient Egypt, the Pharaohs, or rulers, built great pyramids as royal tombs for themselves. The tombs were loaded with gold and other treasure for the Pharaoh to take with him into the afterlife. There was only one little problem . . ."

I could think of more than one little problem at the moment.

"The problem was robbers," said the announcer. "The pyramids were huge. They were visible for miles around. So everyone knew exactly where the pyramids were—and everyone knew there was gold inside."

We had come to the end of the entrance tunnel, which opened onto a narrow hallway. The hallway ran in both directions around the inside of the pyramid. On the wall in front of us, a slide of a pyramid was being projected.

The slides kept changing. One slide showed archaeologists opening a famous tomb. The announcer explained that ancient tomb robbers had found their way into the tomb long before the scientists. When the archaeologists got to the tomb, there wasn't any treasure left.

"The Pharaohs took every precaution possible to safeguard their tombs. They had their scribes carve terrible curses inside the pyramids. The curses warned all intruders of the evil that would befall them if they stepped inside. Some Pharaohs also had their pyramids built with secret traps and dead ends and mazes to foil the robbers. Sometimes the traps worked."

Then the slide showed archaeologists uncovering a skeleton's arm. It belonged to an ancient robber who had been trapped inside a pyramid.

"What a cheerful sight," Casey said.

"Which way should we go?" I said to Gaby.

"Quiet," she said. "I want to see this."

"But—" I began. Then I realized that as long as that guard was standing outside, we were safe from the cavemen and other mannequins. We might as well stay right where we were.

"To give you a feel for how this worked," said the announcer, "the museum is proud to present the Great Pyramid of Hoza Game. This pyramid is fake, but the treasures inside are real. To see the treasures, however, you'll have to solve a few riddles."

"All right!" said Casey.

"Casey," I said, "we don't have time for fun and games."

"Or," the announcer went on, "you can just stay right where you are and get stung by deadly scorpions!"

"On the other hand, maybe you have a point," I told Casey.

"You'll find the riddles on the touch screens, like the one directly ahead of you."

In front of us was a small touch screen with the blinking message TOUCH HERE.

"Have fun," said the announcer. "But remember, if you get a puzzle wrong, you will drop straight down into the pit of deadly scorpions!"

"I wish he'd shut up already about those deadly scorpions," Gaby said.

"So good luck," said the announcer. "I hope you find the treasure—and not the deadly scorpions!"

Casey had already pressed the touch screen. The first image crumbled and new words formed.

Take Up Riddling Now, Robbers, If Getting Hoza's Treasure Is What You Want.

The riddle slowly blinked on and off. Whenever it flashed off, there was a picture of an hourglass instead, with the sand running lower and lower. Under the hourglass was the message: TIME IS RUNNING OUT, TOMB ROBBERS. And underneath that there were pictures of those deadly scorpions. Their stinger tails were curled up over their backs, ready to strike.

"Well," I said, "one good thing is, we don't have to rush. Because those scorpions can't be real."

Then I saw the look on Gaby's face. It made me feel like throwing up. I knew what she was thinking.

"Unless, of course," I went on, "the scorpions have been coming to life like—"

"Like the caveman," Gaby said.

"Uh-oh," I said.

Gaby turned back to the touch screen and repeated the riddle. "Take up riddling now, robbers, if getting Hoza's treasure is what you want . . ."

She didn't say anything more. I looked at Casey. She was staring at the screen all glaze-eyed.

"Well?" I asked.

"We're thinking," Gaby said.

"Well, think out loud," I said. "I'm getting very nervous."

"Uh-oh," Casey said.

I was on edge, as you can imagine. And I had learned through the course of the evening that when Casey said uh-oh, something terrible was about to happen.

"What's wrong?"

"The riddle is going away."

I looked. She was right. A new message formed.

Can I help?

"Ghostwriter?" I said. But there was no way to type back a message on the screen. I took off my Ghostwriter pen and wrote to Ghostwriter on the floor of the passageway.

"HEY, GHOSTWRITER. HECTOR HERE. CAN YOU HELP US SOLVE THIS RIDDLE? TAKE UP RIDDLING NOW, ROBBERS, IF GETTING INTO HOZA'S TREASURE IS WHAT YOU WANT."

Ghostwriter wrote back, The riddle is a little different on screen. Does that matter?

I had forgotten. Ghostwriter already knew the riddle, because he had read the touch screen. I had wasted time. But what did he mean about the riddle being different on the screen? I looked back and forth between what I had written and the message on the screen and I couldn't see anything different at all.

"I think we should go right," Casey said suddenly.

"Why?" I asked.

She shrugged. "Because that's the *right* answer. Get it?"

She smiled sheepishly. It was like the riddles she was always bugging me with, the ones she got from this riddle book she had taken out of the school library. But I didn't think her answer was going to help us much.

"Hey," I said, "if we just go right we have a fifty-fifty chance of not ending up in the scorpion pit."

"You like those odds?" Gaby asked. "I don't," she said. "We've got to solve this."

Casey looked depressed. "I guess I'm better at giving riddles than solving them."

"That's not true," I said. I tried to smile at her. "You can get this one. C'mon!"

We all looked at the touch screen. The hourglass was down to just a handful of grains. There were more pictures of scorpions lashing their tails at us.

"So listen," I said, "what's the deal with scorpions anyway? What happens if they sting you?"

"Hector, there's no time," Gaby snapped. But Gaby can never resist answering a question when she knows the answer. She talked fast. "With some species, it just hurts a lot, like a bee sting. But the ones in the Sahara? When they sting you, you spaz out and die of a heart attack."

We were all silent for about a half a second. Then Casey pointed to the picture of the scorpions on the screen. "What kind are these?"

Gaby didn't have to answer.

"Hurry!" I suddenly cried, which wasn't very helpful, I know, but it just popped out.

Hurry! wrote Ghostwriter on the touch screen. Great minds think alike.

Then the riddle came on for what would probably be the last time. And I finally saw what Ghostwriter meant about how I had written it wrong.

TAKE UP RIDDLING NOW,
ROBBERS, IF GETTING HOZA'S
TREASURE IS WHAT YOU WANT.

"Why are there all those big letters?" I asked.

Casey moved closer, studying the riddle. Then she gave us the biggest smile I'd ever seen and said, "It's like my game! They're initials. T.U.R.N.R.I.G.H.T. Turn right!"

We turned right.

And not a second too soon. Just then the platform where we'd been standing and the platform to the left slowly sank out of sight. Down below we heard little snapping sounds.

"I hope that's just a tape recording of those scorpions," Gaby said.

"Let's not stick around and find out!" I started

70

running down the passageway to the right. I didn't get far. It was a dead end.

There was another touch screen blinking at us. TOUCH HERE.

I smacked it with my fist.

DON'T WORRY, VANDALS. 1 BRICK IS GOOD. JUST TOUCH IT AND YOU WILL FIND MUCH GOLD.
BUT IF YOU TOUCH A BAD BRICK, YOU WILL TOUCH A SCORPION'S TAIL.
THINK HARD, LAZY-BRAINS. ACT QUICKLY. AND DON'T ALLOW US TO OUTFOX YOU.
AFTER ALL, A SCORPION'S STING IS FATAL.

The riddle disappeared almost at once, as Ghost-writer wrote,

Is this just for fun? I worry . . .

"WE'RE WORRIED TOO," I wrote back on the floor.

"The bricks have letters on them," Gaby announced.

"D.W.V.1.B.I.G.J.T.I.A.Y.W.F.M.G.," Casey said.

"What's *that*?" I asked.

"Those are the initials of all the words in the first

three sentences of the riddle," she said. She frowned. "I guess it's not the same kind of riddle."

"I.G.N.," I said.

The frown turned into a grin. "I guess not," said Casey.

"Guys," Gaby said. "We'd better solve *this* riddle."

We all looked at the bricks in the three walls of the dead end. They were lettered A to Z. I had no idea which one to touch. Which were the bad bricks? Which was the good one?

"Hey!" Gaby said.

The letters on the touch screen were glowing green as Ghostwriter lifted them into the air and spun them.

```
Ar  any of th  bricks brok n? Mayb
it m ans bad in th  s ns  of brok n?
```

"Great," I said. "Now Ghostwriter is giving us extra puzzles."

But Casey was sounding out the words. "Are any of the bricks broken? Maybe it means bad in the sense of broken?"

"Way to go, Casey!" cheered Gaby.

I clapped her on the back. She had deciphered Ghostwriter's message perfectly.

Then we studied the bricks.

Every single one looked new and perfect. Not a crack in the bunch.

"Maybe there's a clue in the way they used the number one," Gaby said. She peered around at the bricks. "Are there any bricks with numbers on them?"

"Nope," said Casey. "They all have letters."

I glanced at the touch screen. The hourglass was running low again.

"Wait a minute," I said. "Great Sphin."

"Wrong clue," Gaby said.

"I know," I said. "But maybe it's the same idea. Ghostwriter left out a letter that time. Why? Because he didn't have it around to use."

"Now he has the whole alphabet," Casey pointed out, gesturing at the bricks.

By then, Ghostwriter's message had evaporated into nothing. I was picturing it in my mind's eye. "Ar any of th bricks brokn?" I repeated. I sounded like I was lisping. "He left out the *E*!" I cried.

Gaby rushed back to the touch screen. "You're right," she said, studying the riddle. "They didn't use the letter *E* in the riddle, not even once. Even though *E* is the most commonly used letter in the English language. So that's why they used the numeral one instead of the word! To keep from using the letter *E*!"

"But," said Casey, "he had an *E* right here."

She was pointing to a brick. It was stamped with a big *E*.

"I know," I said. "But he didn't get the letters from the bricks. He lifted them off the touch screen. That brick you're pointing at, that must be the one good brick!"

"Touch it," Gaby ordered Casey.

On the touch screen, the last grains of sand were sifting down onto the snapping scorpions.

"This one?" Casey asked, her fingertips just millimeters away from the E-brick.

"T.O.," I said with a big smile.

Which was probably the single stupidest thing I've ever said in my entire life.

Because, instead of touching *E*, Casey moved her hand and touched bricks T and O. And then the trapdoor opened beneath our feet and we were all falling.

Down, down, down . . .

Down into the pit of deadly scorpions.

chapter
nine

I landed face-first in the dark pit.

Right away I could feel the scorpions wriggling all around me. I could feel the little creatures with my hands. Feel them on my face!

I flailed my arms wildly. It was too late. One sting would have been enough to kill me. I felt the scorpions stinging my face, my back, my neck, my hands, my legs, my feet. I smacked into something.

"Help! They're stinging me!" I heard Gaby scream.

I opened my mouth to scream as well but I got a mouthful of bugs.

I spat them out as hard as I could. I was holding a bunch in each fist. I was starting to spaz out, just as Gaby had predicted. I was shaking like a madman. And then—

Someone grabbed me with both hands and tried

to hold me still. Casey. She was yelling something. It sounded like "Not real!"

And then, I don't know how, but it began to seep into my brain that I wasn't getting stung.

I looked down at the bugs in my fist, holding them close to my eyes to see them in the dark.

The bugs were plastic. They weren't real scorpions at all. And I was the one who had stung Gaby, scratching her face when I was flailing around.

I sat up. So did Gaby and Casey. They both had creepy crawlers stuck to their hair, their faces, their clothes. We had dropped down into a big vat of the stuff, like those huge tents filled with Nerf balls that they sometimes have at amusement parks.

"Sorry," said the announcer over a loudspeaker. "You have lost the Game of Hoza. But don't feel too bad. You still get to see . . . the treasure."

There was a sign labeled TREASURE and an arrow pointing the way.

"Well, that's clear enough," Gaby said with a laugh.

She climbed out of the vat of plastic scorpions. Casey and I followed.

"Now that we're all still alive," Gaby said, brushing off the plastic bugs, "do you mind telling me why you told Casey to push T and O?"

"I meant T.O., That One," I said, feeling very embarrassed.

"Y.D.T.D." Gaby said. "You Deserved To Die."

We went down a narrow passageway that opened into a large room. Suddenly I felt as if the floor had dropped out from underneath me all over again.

The room was dazzling and bright. In the middle sat a big stone coffin with a gold lid. The lid was open. King Hoza's mummy was lying inside. All around the walls were glass cases filled with gold trinkets. And lined up on the far wall, bowing down to their king, were the ten little gold statues.

"We're rich," I said.

"It's so beautiful," said Gaby. The gold was dancing in her dark eyes.

Casey walked over to the coffin.

"Careful," I said.

"Are you sleeping, King Hoza?" Casey asked. She stepped closer.

"Casey," warned Gaby. "Don't touch."

"Why? The guard said we could."

"But there's a sign."

The sign said DON'T TOUCH.

Still, Casey reached out a hand and touched the king's golden beard. She stroked his cheek. And then the mummy's eyes opened.

King Hoza sprang out of his coffin!

chapter
ten

King Hoza's mummy-eyes glowed bright red and evil!

Casey turned and raced back to where we were standing. The mummy opened his mouth and laughed. He turned his head slowly from side to side.

By then, I had realized that it was just a robot, part of the exhibit.

The announcer's voice came back on the loud-speakers. "Sorry, we couldn't resist giving you a little scare. Don't worry. King Hoza isn't coming back to life."

"That's easy for you to say," Gaby mumbled.

"As you can see," the announcer said, "we buried King Hoza with ten solid-gold sun worshipers, all bowing down as they greet the rising sun."

"There," Gaby said, pointing to the little gold worshipers.

"And folks," said the announcer, "believe me. Those gold statues are real."

"Think of how much candy you could buy with one of those, Hector," Gaby joked.

"Yeah," I said. "Ten or twenty candy bars at least."

"Thank you for visiting the Great Pyramid of Hoza," the announcer said. "This concludes our tour. Please make room for the next group of spectators."

"No way," I said. "We're staying right here where we're safe."

Casey was taking off her backpack. She took out a notebook. Then she took off her Ghostwriter pen.

"What are you up to?" I asked her.

"I'm starting a Caseybook," she said.

"A what?"

Gaby was laughing. "A Caseybook! I like that."

"Oh," I said. "A *case*book."

"Duh," said Casey without looking up.

I felt myself reddening. "What do we need a casebook for?" I asked. I guess I was trying to get her back.

"Maybe it will help us figure out how to stop those creatures out there," Casey said.

"That's a good idea," Gaby said, before I could tell Casey it was a dumb one. Frankly, I didn't see how a casebook could help us. After all, we were up against supernatural monsters, not criminals.

Casey started making notes on everything that had happened so far. Ghostwriter was reading right along, too. The green glow was swirling around her pen like crazy, sending off sparks.

Thank you, Ghostwriter, I thought. The ghost knew we were in serious trouble. He was working hard to help.

"This is a good idea," I admitted, "because now Ghostwriter will be up to date on everything that's going on."

Casey looked up at me and gave me one of those dazzling smiles of hers.

Then Gaby and I started chiming in with all the details we could remember from things that we had seen so far. T. R. galloping on his statue. The Indian bride with nine bracelets on a single wrist.

"I don't know," I said, feeling unsure again, "are all these details important?"

"Sure," Gaby said. "You never know where the clues are going to be. Every detail counts. Try to remember every single thing."

I closed my eyes and did just that. I remembered that Iroquois Indian in the longhouse. I remembered studying him through the glass, from the tip of his head-feathers to the shoelaces on his—

I opened my eyes.

"Gaby?"

"What?"

"Do moccasins have shoelaces?"

"I don't know. Why?"

"Because that Indian in the exhibit had shoelaces on his moccasins. I remember that now."

"Thank you for visiting the Great Pyramid of Hoza," the announcer voice repeated. "This concludes our tour. *Please* make room for the next group of spectators."

We ignored him. "Maybe the people who make the exhibits made a mistake," said Casey.

Gaby tilted her head to one side, thinking about it. "I don't know. I think they're very careful about that kind of stuff at the museum, trying to be accurate and all. I mean, that's the whole point of a place like this. Anyway, write it down on a special page marked *clues*."

Casey wrote CLUES at the top of a new page, then underlined it. She wrote, *Shoelaces on moccasins.*

Then she reached into her pocket and took out the piece of paper she had found in the hall. "Clue number two," she said proudly, unfolding it.

We all looked at it.

H.O.A.E.

G.S.

#1

11:45 - 12:30   T.R.
12:30 - 1:00   1st floor
1:00 - 1:45   3rd floor
1:45 - 2:15   T.R.

#2

11:45 - 12:15   T.R.
12:15 - 12:45   4th floor
12:45 - 1:15   T.R.
1:15 - 2:00   T.R.

#3

11:45 - 12:15   1st floor
12:15 - 12:45   T.R.

#3

12:45 - 1:15   2nd floor
1:15 - 1:45   T.R.

#4

11:30 - 12:30   3rd floor
12:30 - 1:00   T.R.
1:00 - 1:30   1st floor
1:30 - 2:00   4th floor

#5

11:45 - 12:15   4th floor
12:15 - 12:45   3rd floor
12:45 - 1:15   2nd floor
1:15 - 2:15   T.R.

"I really don't think that piece of paper has anything to do with our problems," I said.

"You never know," Gaby said.

"*I* know," I said.

"H.O.A.E.," Gaby said, reading the headline on the page and ignoring me. "That sounds like one of your riddles, Casey."

"Howard Owns Absolutely Everything," Casey guessed.

"He Orders Awful Eggs," guessed Gaby.

I was feeling like a drag just standing there and

not playing. So I said, "Henry Often Acts Egg-headed."

Casey giggled. Then she wrote what was going on in her "Caseybook" for Ghostwriter. He spun back a guess of his own.

Hold on. Answer Eventually.

"You know what we're forgetting?" Gaby said. "We have to think about where it came from. Just like in your riddles, Casey, where we had to fit the words into the sentence."

"This came from the floor," Casey said.

"In the museum," I said.

"Yeah!" Casey agreed. "H.O.A.E. is probably some place in the museum."

"So we just have to go over the names of the rooms!" I said.

Gaby's eyes were shining. "Ghostwriter was right. We held on and soon we had a plan."

"Hall," Casey shouted out.

"Hall of," I said.

It was like we were three parts of one person, be-cause Gaby finished the clue. "Hall of Ancient Egypt!"

"Okay," I said. "So far so good." I pointed at the next part of the schedule. "Now G.S."

Casey wrote down the puzzle for Ghostwriter.

S could stand for schedule, he suggested.

84

"EXCELLENT!" Casey wrote back. "I BET THAT'S IT! YOU'RE SO SMART, GHOST-WRITER."

Thank you, Ghostwriter wrote back, and then the letters all folded over in the middle, as Ghost-writer took a little bow. We all laughed.

"G. Schedule," said Gaby. "Good Schedule. Great Schedule. Guard Schedule."

"Guard Schedule!" we all cried in unison, because right away we knew that was it.

"The guard said there are five guards on duty to-night," I pointed out, "and look. One two three four five."

"We're geniuses," Gaby said, glowing.

"What else can we tell from this schedule?" I wondered out loud.

"It's written in pencil," Casey said.

I was about to say that that was obvious, but then I realized that Casey had made another excellent point. "So that means it's probably not official," I said.

"Yeah," Casey said. "More like somebody just copied it down."

"And they only copied part of the night sched-ule," said Gaby.

"T.R.," I said, pointing to the initials on the schedule.

Casey gave me a look and I winked at her. She was right. That game of hers was sure coming in handy. I snapped my fingers. "Teddy Roosevelt! The statue of that guy on the horse in front of the museum!"

"Why would they have to guard that statue?" Casey wondered.

She had a point. My guess didn't feel right to me anymore.

"Tomb Room," Gaby gasped.

"Yes!" I said. And we high-fived, all three of us at once.

Casey turned to the clue page and started writing down what we had figured out. Then she tucked the schedule into the back of the notepad where we could get at it later if we needed.

As it turned out, we needed it right away. Gaby said, "Wait a minute! Let me see that again!"

"What?" I asked. "What? What? What?"

"Stop saying what," Gaby said with a little smile, "and let me think."

I let her think.

"I just wanted to make sure," she said, "that there are guards out there all the time. Otherwise, this pyramid might not be such a good hiding place. It might be more like a death trap."

"I wish you hadn't said that," I said.

I was studying the schedule over Casey's shoulder. I breathed a sigh of relief. "There's a guard on duty at all times, at least until two in the morning."

Two in the morning. Normally, I would have

been long asleep by then. Right now, I'd never felt so awake in my entire life.

"There were two guards when we came in," Casey reminded us.

Gaby traced her finger down the schedule. "Maybe there are always two guards."

"Nope," Casey said. "Look. Right here. There's a gap from one o'clock to one-fifteen, when there's only one guard."

"Good work," I said, though I didn't know what it meant.

Gaby looked at her watch. "So the gap starts—"

A door swung open in the wall of the Tomb Room.

In rushed a caveman with an ax, a bride in a gold headdress, Ndzingi the giant, and an Iroquois Indian with a knife.

"Now," squeaked Gaby.

eleven

We ran the only way we could, which was around King Hoza and back into the room with the scorpions. It was a dumb way to go, because that room was a dead end.

The creatures chased us. We kept running, circling around the big scorpion pit and going back into the golden Tomb Room. So it wasn't such a dumb idea after all, because now the creatures were behind us. And the door to freedom lay ahead.

"Thank you for visiting the Great Pyramid of Hoza," the announcer voice was droning. "This concludes our tour. *Please* make room for the next group of spectators."

This time I was more than glad to obey. We practically flew out of the room. I could feel the creatures right behind me. One of them was reaching for me.

I could feel its fingers closing around the back of my shirt collar—

The cloth of my shirt slipped out of its grasp.

Speaking of slipping—

The caveman was barefoot, but the Iroquois Indian had those moccasins on. They must have been slippery, because he went down. There was a loud grunt of pain as the caveman crashed into the Indian and toppled over as well. Which meant that they were blocking the way for the giant and the bride. We didn't look back to see what happened next; we just kept running.

And running.

Down the narrow twisting passageway, which led to—

Another touch screen.

The sign on the wall said LEFT OR RIGHT?

"Oh no!" Casey whispered.

Gaby slammed the touch screen with both hands.

THE FINAL RIDDLE
IF YOU MAKE A WRONG TURN,
YOU'LL BE LEFT OUT.

"Right!" mouthed Gaby, before I even had time to start to solve the riddle.

I decided to take her word for it. We raced right, going so fast we almost slipped as well.

Gaby must have solved the riddle correctly, because the path led straight out of the pyramid. At first I couldn't tell where we were, then I saw we had come out all the way on the other side of the pyramid from where we had come in. I started running again. I was running through the narrow space in back of the pyramid, right along the wall of the room. Gaby and Casey followed.

"You know what?" Gaby said as we ran. "I just . . . thought of something . . . that riddle . . . it could mean left or right."

The riddle was repeating itself in my brain. *If you make a wrong turn, you'll be left out.* I saw what she meant. *Left out*—you could take that to mean that turning left was the way out. Maybe both answers were correct.

That would explain why, as we ran around the back of the pyramid, the caveman, the Iroquois Indian, the giant, and the bride were all waiting for us.

chapter
twelve

It was dark behind the pyramid, so the creatures seemed to appear out of nowhere.

I ran smack into the bare-chested Iroquois Indian. That was enough to knock the wind right out of me. I can tell you, that's a really awful feeling, in case you're lucky enough never to have had it happen to you. It feels like your lungs are broken. You can't breathe, you just wheeze and think *I'm dying.*

On top of which, the Indian had me in a bear hug. He lifted me off the ground like a mail package Jamal's grandmother CeCe might deliver to somebody's doorstep. I heard Casey and Gaby shouting and screaming and caught glimpses of them struggling. It looked like they were putting up a better fight than I had. Casey must have bitten the caveman because he moaned loudly. But it was all over in a few seconds. At least I didn't hear any more struggling. Casey's and Gaby's shouts got all muffled and quiet, as if the creatures had clapped their hands over their mouths.

The Iroquois Indian carried me down the hall. Finally I got my lungs working again and started to kick and buck. But the man just squeezed harder and knocked the wind right out of me again.

You might be wondering what goes through a kid's mind when something that used to be made out of wood comes alive and kidnaps him. I can tell you. Not a whole lot. It's happening. It's real. You don't have time to think how amazing it all is.

The Iroquois Indian carried me over to a big Eskimo exhibit. At the Natural History Museum of New York, there are little doors next to the exhibits. You might not even notice them if you aren't looking for them. It's where the museum's artists go when they want to change something in the exhibit, say, or reglue some tiger's drooping whiskers.

The Iroquois Indian dropped me on the floor outside the exhibit door with a thump. I banged my head pretty hard. I tried to get up, but he had me pinned against the door with his legs. Those legs were even stronger than those arms.

He was using his knife on the little door's lock, trying to pick it. He got it opened. Then he snatched me up and carried me inside.

From the outside, it had looked freezing inside the Eskimo exhibit. A bunch of Eskimo mannequins were huddled around an igloo, fishing in a hole in the ice, warming their hands around a fire. Inside, though, the air was just the same temperature as outside. I was glad to see that the Eskimos weren't moving. So not all the mannequins were coming to life. That was some relief. Tiny, but some.

The Indian dropped me in the back of the exhibit. I tried to get to my feet, but he put one moccasin on the small of my back and pushed me down. Then he grabbed my hands and held them together behind my back. The next thing I knew my hands were being lashed together tightly with what felt like leather strips.

I could hear a lot of commotion in the exhibit. Either Gaby and Casey were joining me, or the Eskimos were. I prayed it was Gaby and Casey.

"Sir . . . we don't . . . mean any harm," I said. But my face was pressed down against the dusty floor and my words were muffled. "We were just visiting the museum. We didn't mean to stare at you. Is that why you're so mad at us? Hey, I guess it doesn't feel good, standing still all year and having kids peer at you and bang on the glass. But, please . . . let us— Ow!—go."

I thought I heard the Indian snicker. Then he pulled my knots tighter and went to work on tying my legs together.

And then he was gone.

I rolled over and worked my way into a sitting

position, which is not the easiest thing to do with your hands tied behind your back and your feet tied together. I ended up rubbing my face in the floor but good. I'm surprised I didn't give myself a nosebleed. I also skinned my elbows and ground dust into my clothes.

I looked around. In back of the igloo, where the public can't see, there was no decoration. There were metal poles holding up the exhibit. And there lay Casey. She had a terrified look on her face. She had been tied up better than I had, the rope lashed around one of the poles.

It wasn't the way she was tied that had her so scared. They had tied her up about an inch from the head of a huge polar bear. If that bear came to life, the first thing he'd see would be Casey, and he'd probably be hungry after a year of not eating.

"Don't worry," I told her. "This exhibit hasn't come to life yet."

I know that wasn't the most comforting news in the world, but Casey managed to give me a weak smile.

I inched myself around so that I could get a look at the rest of our prison. I started to scream.

There was an Eskimo sitting right next to me. He had his head down. He was frozen in the act of skinning a fish with a sharp knife.

Sure, he was frozen *now*. But the caveman had

had his head down earlier in the evening, and then he had looked right at me.

I heard movement in the shadows of the exhibit and craned my head to see. I was praying that it wasn't going to be the polar bear padding toward me.

It wasn't. It was Gaby, groaning in frustration as she tried to get out of her ropes. But, like Casey, she was tied too tightly.

"Gaby," I called. "You okay?"

Gaby stopped struggling. "Yeah," she said.

She didn't look okay. She had scratches all over her face.

Then I remembered, the scratches were from me, back in the vat of scorpions.

I tried to think of a way out.

Just then, on the glass front of the exhibit, I saw letters dancing. It was Ghostwriter, using the signs outside the exhibit to write to us.

Are you okay?
I sense great danger.
I'm very worried.
How can I help?

Since he was writing on the other side of the glass, his messages were coming out backward. So it took me a moment to decode them.

Are you okay?
I sense great danger.
I'm very worried.
How can I help?

I pulled my hands hard against the ropes, but they only seemed to tighten, like a slipknot, cutting off my circulation.

Ghostwriter is an incredible friend. He's gotten us out of all sorts of horrible scrapes and helped us solve lots of mysteries. But if I couldn't write to him, there was no way to communicate with him. He couldn't hear.

I tried flipping my Ghostwriter pen up in the air. My plan was to catch it in my teeth. I even managed to do it once. But I couldn't get the pen open.

There was no sound in the exhibit now. Gaby was resting after another bout of struggling against her ropes. Casey was tied so tight she couldn't move. And I was thinking.

What I was thinking was . . .

What was that slithering sound I was hearing?

"Hector?" Casey asked quietly.

Gaby had started to struggle again, but now she stopped. "Do you hear that?" she asked.

I could feel all the tiny hairs that I didn't even know I had standing straight up on the back of my neck.

"Hector?" Casey said again, louder this time.

"Okay," I said. "We've got *un poco de problema.*" When I get really upset, sometimes I talk in Spanish without even knowing it.

"It's a snake, right?" Casey asked.

"Sí."

"It must be from the Herpetology Department," Gaby said, struggling hard.

"Sí," I said again. I was trying hard to think, but it was very difficult when I was watching a snake slither in a little S-shape around the exhibit's small fishing hole. The snake was heading right toward us.

I turned and looked again at the Eskimo man sitting next to me. "What about you?" I asked him. "You got any ideas?"

Just that same blank stare, as he looked down at the sharp knife in his hands.

The knife glinted, like it was winking at me. And then I knew what to do.

"¡Dios mi! I've got an idea!"

"Hector," Casey said, and there was pleading in her voice. I glanced over and saw why. The snake was wriggling right at her.

I slid myself around so that I was sitting right in front of the Eskimo. Then I backed up, trying to feel with my hands for the sharp knife, trying to rub the ropes against the blade. With my luck, I figured I would slice my hands off. Well, that would be one way to get out of the ropes!

I found the blade. I started to saw my hands slowly back and forth. I could tell the blade was sharp, but the Eskimo's jointed arms were bending away from the pressure I was putting on the knife. At this rate, I'd never get the ropes cut.

Feeling foolish and still with my back turned, I started whispering. "Listen, Mr. Eskimo? Hello? I'm very sorry to bother you like this. But I need your help. Uh, I know we're disturbing your home and everything—"

"Hector," I heard Gaby mutter, "if this is your plan, then we're dead meat."

I ignored her. "The thing is, Mr. Eskimo—"

"Hector," Gaby interrupted me again. "Most Eskimos call themselves Inuit. It means 'the people' in their language."

"What are you talking about?"

"In the 1970s many Eskimo tribes changed their name to Inuit."

I was pretty sure that *this* man hadn't heard about any name change, but I wasn't going to take chances. "Okay, Mr. Inuit, sorry about that. Anyway, here's the deal. We don't know why that caveman and that giant and that Iroquois Indian and that bride are all so mad at us. But I promise you, we didn't do anything wrong. We're just schoolkids. I'm Hector Carrero. And that's Gaby Fernandez over there. She's a really great person. And so is Casey. Anyway, if you help us out of here, I promise I'll donate my milk money for a whole week to the museum."

"*Hector!*" Casey cried.

I didn't have to look to know that that snake was really close to her. But I couldn't think about that now. Casey, my teammate and my friend, was in terrible trouble. But the only way I could help her was if I kept my mind on what I was doing.

I was sweating all over. I kept talking to the Inuit man. "So what I'm going to do is, I'm going to keep trying to rub my ropes against your knife. And if you could help out by just keeping the knife pressed up against the ropes really tight—"

As I spoke I was pushing the ropes against the knife and suddenly I could feel pressure. It was as if the Inuit were pressing back with the weapon.

More than that. As I moved my hands one way, he seemed to move the knife the other. I could hear the sawing sound. I could feel the knife going through the ropes.

And seconds later, my hands were free.

Which was good, because the snake was now sliding across Casey's face.

c h a p t e r
thirteen

I got to my feet, almost losing my balance several times because my feet were tied together so tightly. I grabbed a fishing spear out of the hands of one of the Inuit women. "Thanks," I said. "I'll bring it right back."

Then I hopped over to Casey. The snake had crawled over her face and was curled up next to her arm. I placed the point of the spear right under the slithering snake's belly. Then I flicked the spear. There was a hiss as the snake flew along the floor and ended up somewhere in back.

I figured that the snake would return soon. First I cut my legs free. Then I worked frantically at Casey's ropes with the edge of the spear, cutting with all my might.

When I got her hands free I gave her the spear so she could work on her leg ropes. Then I borrowed the knife from the Inuit who had helped set me free. "Just for one second," I told him. Then I started working on Gaby.

I heard this loud angry rattling from the snake. I was so scared I dragged her halfway through the exhibit.

"Don't worry about the snake!" Gaby cried. "Just get the ropes. Rattlers usually flee from danger."

"I'm the same way," I said. But what I was thinking about was one word she had said: *usually.* I hid Gaby behind the igloo and went to work on the ropes as hard and fast as I could.

By then Casey had gotten free. She came over to help me. We had Gaby out of her ropes in no time.

"Let's go!" cried Gaby.

"Just a second," I said.

"Where are you going?" Casey shrieked at me.

I didn't answer. I just grabbed her spear and ran back into the exhibit. I slipped the knife and the spear back into the Inuits' wooden hands. *"Muchas gracias,"* I said. "Uh, that means thanks a lot." I added that because I didn't know if the Inuit people spoke Spanish. "You saved our lives," I said.

Then I turned and ran.

We headed for the museum's front exit. We didn't bother to look to see if anyone was hiding around any corners, either. This time we just ran flat out. Down the steps. Down the hall. Down to the lobby where we first came in.

And right into the arms of the cavemen.

"Hey, slow down," one of the cavemen said.

"It's okay," said another caveman. "We brought Lieutenant McQuade with us."

I was trying to pull away from the caveman who was holding me. "Hector," the caveman said, "chill, man! It's me!"

After everything we had been through, chilling was no longer in my vocabulary. But the light was beginning to dawn. These weren't the *cavemen*-cavemen. These were Alex, Jamal, Lenni, and Tina—in cavemen costumes!

I looked around the dark lobby. One of the front doors was open. So why hadn't the alarm sounded? Then I saw muscle-bound security guard number 4. That was why. He must have let my friends in. The guard was talking with Lieutenant McQuade.

The caveman who'd been holding me now lifted

his papier-mâché mask. Underneath was Jamal's friendly face. "Ghostwriter brought us Casey's casebook notes," he whispered to me. "So we knew you guys weren't kidding."

Another caveman lifted her mask. Tina! "We ran over here as fast as we could," she told us.

"Yeah," said Lenni, lifting her mask. "We ran so fast we lost Mr. Fernandez."

Alex and Gaby's father had gone to the parade to make sure Alex and the others would be okay.

"Papa'll catch up," said a voice I recognized as Alex's. "Are you guys okay?"

"I guess so," I said. I looked at Casey and Gaby. I could see they felt the same way I did. We were all so relieved to have our friends here—and the police—that we were in a kind of daze. It took me a second to remember we were in the middle of a huge emergency.

"You're going to need more cops!" I called loudly to Lieutenant McQuade. "The whole museum is coming to life. Bring the Marines. Nuke the building!"

Lieutenant McQuade held up a hand. "Don't worry, Hector. We're going to get this all under control. I'll be right with you."

Finally he came over.

"The guard here says you guys have been getting pretty upset tonight."

Right away all three of us, Gaby and Casey and I, starting talking at once again. You know what that sounds like by now, so I won't bother to write it out.

Lieutenant McQuade has helped us on lots of cases. He knows that we have provided the police with very valuable information for catching criminals. He doesn't know how we get that info of course, since he doesn't know about Ghostwriter. But he trusts us.

Except this time he looked very doubtful.

"Guys," he said, "I'd love to help you out here, but you're telling me a caveman statue came to life and chased you with an ax. And then this caveman statue tied you up? And then a wooden Inuit man cut you out of the ropes?"

He glanced back at the security guard. "Did these kids get anything to eat tonight?"

Alex raised his mask. "Lieutenant McQuade? If they say the exhibits are coming to life, we have to believe them. They're my teammates, sir. If they say it's true, it's true."

The other cavemen chorused their agreement. I glanced around at the five cavemen. I felt like hugging each and every one of them.

Lieutenant McQuade said to the security guard, "Let me borrow that walkie-talkie for a moment, would you? I want to talk to each one of the guards, hear if they've seen anything strange tonight."

The guard sighed, like he was sure this was a big waste of time. But he handed over the walkie-talkie. Lieutenant McQuade punched the talk button.

Just then—

One of my very own team members knocked the walkie-talkie out of Lieutenant McQuade's hand with a stone ax.

McQuade shouted in surprise.

So did I. I was so confused at that moment, I felt like my brain was splitting in two. I think I had the idea that maybe my friends had turned into cavemen because they were wearing such realistic cavemen costumes. I mean, after the night I had had, I was willing to believe anything. But then, an instant later, it hit me.

Five cavemen, *four* team members?

One of the exhibits had joined our group!

And now here came the Iroquois Indian, lunging out of the shadows to klonk the guard on the head.

And the next thing I knew there was the clinking sound of jewelry and the bride was rushing past us. And then Ndzingi the giant shoved me hard. I went down.

"Stop them!" Gaby yelled.

But it was too late.

The four mannequins rushed out the open door and were gone.

fifteen

I ran after them. Casey and Gaby were right behind me, and so were my other teammates, the four cavemen. And behind them came Lieutenant McQuade.

But when I came out onto the museum steps, I stopped short. For one half-second I was probably more scared than I had been at any other time that night, including when the rattlesnake was coming to get us.

The street was jam-packed with noisy, bizarre-looking monsters. Ghosts, goblins, elves, zombies, werewolves, witches—

Gaby banged into me from behind and almost fell. When she saw the look on my face, she grabbed me, pulling me down the steps after her. "It's the parade!" she yelled. "The parade!"

Ohhhhhhhhhhhhhhhh . . . the Halloween parade.

That was a relief, to say the least.

But in the street I could see four real monsters—a caveman, a giant, an Iroquois Indian, and a bride—all blending in with the crowd of people in their costumes. We ran after them. Alex and Jamal, who had started out behind me, were now racing on ahead.

To tell you the truth, I wasn't running my fastest. I was pretty exhausted, and part of me didn't want to catch up with the mannequins. Let them go, I figured. But I forced myself to keep running.

At least, I ran until I reached the street. The parade was so jam-packed, there was no way you could run through it. You could barely walk. Right away I got separated from the group and Lieutenant McQuade. Everywhere I turned, people were knocking into me or stepping on me. Somebody dressed as a bee poked me in the back of the head with her stinger. Then a pumpkin bumped me so hard I almost fell over.

I saw Casey up ahead. She was looking back for me, this wild look in her eye. Casey's pretty short. She looked like she might get trampled.

Lenni had taken off her mask. "Here!" she yelled to Casey. She lifted Casey up onto her shoulders. "Do you see them?"

Casey searched the crowd, then pointed up ahead and screamed, *"There!"*

You would think someone screaming would cause

quite a big ruckus. Not in the Manhattan Halloween Parade. *Everyone* was screaming and laughing and acting loco. I was lucky I heard Casey. I tried to move ahead as fast as I could, saying *"Perdón, Perdón,"* and "Excuse me, excuse me, *por favor,"* about ten million times.

I spotted Tina. She had her mask off. She was swinging her arms hard, trying to power-walk through the crowd.

A hand grabbed my arm. It was Gaby. We worked our way up ahead together.

And then I saw the caveman.

My eyes locked on his back like a heat-seeking missile.

I was in luck. Because just then we hit a pocket of space where the crowd wasn't so thick so we could jog forward.

Casey was screaming, "Get him! Get him!"

Jamal came from one side. Tina from the other. Then Gaby and I arrived. Followed almost instantly by Lenni and Casey, who dropped down from Lenni's shoulders. So we all tackled that caveman like you would crumple a soda can with a truck.

We had him!

chapter
sixteen

"Hey! Let me up! What are you doing? Get off me!"

His voice was very tiny at first, because we were all piled on top of him. But after a few moments I realized who we had tackled.

Alex.

Since he was in the lead and wearing a caveman costume, we had gotten confused. "It's Alex!" I started shouting. "Let him up!" But we were all tangled together like a pretzel, and getting up wasn't so easy. I heard people in the parade laughing at us as they walked by. They probably thought we were just playing around.

When we finally got up off the ground, we tried to keep searching for the mannequins. I figured they had gotten too much of a head start by now, but we kept looking for several blocks. We did find one more caveman. But when Jamal grabbed it, she started screaming in a shrill voice.

Turned out this was somebody's *abuela*—I mean, grandma—who had dressed up in a caveman suit to make her grandson happy on Halloween. She was really upset.

Jamal kept apologizing, but just then a policeman made his way through the crowd toward us. I was praying it would be Lieutenant McQuade. It wasn't.

"We thought she was a *real* caveman," Casey explained to the cop.

Which, as you can imagine, did not help our situation too much.

In the end, after about ten minutes' more explaining by me and the rest of the group, the cop still didn't believe a word we were saying. He insisted on taking us back to the museum. He wanted to talk to Lieutenant McQuade personally.

When we got back to the museum lobby, the guard was still there—with Mr. Fernandez. But they had no idea where Lieutenant McQuade was. Mr. Fernandez was very glad to be reunited with his children and their friends. He was not so glad to see that we were with a policeman.

"They tackled some poor old woman," the cop explained.

Mr. Fernandez clapped his hand against his forehead. He looked very angry.

The security guard was looking even more furious.

He kept rubbing his head. It looked like he had a bad bump. "Okay," he said, arms crossed, "which one of you brats knocked me on the head?"

At first, I didn't know what he was talking about. It turned out that in all the crazy commotion, the guard hadn't seen the mannequins run out of the museum. He just thought that *we* conked him one and ran for it!

When he said that, the cop got even madder. And as if that wasn't enough people who were mad at us, in walked Mr. Cepeda and the six other kids on the trip. They were led by another security guard, the bald guy, number 2.

"There you are," Mr. Cepeda said when he saw me. He was shaking his head over and over again, like he was too mad to say anything more.

"Mr. Cepeda! Where have you been?" Casey cried.

"Where have we been?" Mr. Cepeda asked softly. I could tell he was about to explode. I had never seen him like this, not even the time Carlos left the lab windows open and all those pigeons got in and wrecked a seed experiment the class had been working on.

"We were 'accidentally' locked in the Bird Room," Mr. Cepeda said, fuming. "Very funny joke."

"Wow," Gaby said. "One of the exhibits must have done it."

"Uh-huh," Mr. Cepeda said, turning so red I thought he was going to have a stroke. "Hector, Gaby, Casey—I have to admit. The three of you pulling a crazy stunt like this . . . I-I never would have believed it."

"You think *we* did it?" Gaby asked, amazed.

"Did what?" I asked.

"He thinks we locked them in," Casey said.

"Who else did it?" Alicia called from across the lobby. "The Inuits?"

That was a very real possibility, but I wasn't going to try to explain that to them.

"I don't even know where the Bird Room is," Gaby said.

"It's right here on the first floor," Patrick said, "and you're lying."

"Gaby," Mr. Fernandez said sharply. And then he let fly with this wild stream of Spanish. I could translate it, but I don't think Mr. Fernandez would want me to.

When he was done, Gaby looked like she was going to cry, which is a rare sight, let me tell you. Alex put his arm around her shoulders. Jamal put his arm around Casey. Lenni and Tina didn't put their arms around me, but they stood right nearby. It was times like this when it really felt great being part of a team.

"I don't believe this," I said to no one in particular. "Has anyone walked around the museum and seen what's going on?"

"Oh, yeah," security guard number 2 told us. "We've checked the entire museum, son—not that your crazy story deserved that kind of treatment, believe me. And there's no sign of anything stirring. All the exhibits are right where they always were."

"They are?" Casey asked.

"I want these kids arrested," guard number 4 said to the cop. "I think I have a concussion."

Arrested!

The word had a chilling effect on the team.

And everyone was just staring at us—staring with furious scowls.

Me, I'm usually a big talker. But right then, I couldn't think of a single word to say.

Just when I thought we were safe, we had gotten into a whole new kind of trouble.

chapter
seventeen

Mr. Cepeda was having a little meeting with Mr. Fernandez and the cop and the security guards. It was not fun watching them talk. They kept glancing at us. And all of them were shaking their heads. What were they doing? Trying to think of some horrible torture for us?

The rest of the class stayed on the other side of the lobby, scowling at us. I stuck my tongue out at Carlos. He just rolled his eyes.

"I can't believe they don't believe us," Casey said, stamping her foot.

"Well," Lenni said in a low voice, "you gotta admit, it is a pretty wild story."

"Yeah," Alex agreed. "If we weren't your teammates, I wouldn't believe it either."

"Can I see the casebook?" Tina asked.

Casey handed it over. "You believe me, don't you, Tina?" she asked.

"Well," Tina said thoughtfully, "I believe you guys saw what you say you saw. But maybe . . ."

"Maybe *what*?" I demanded.

"I don't know, maybe there's another explanation."

At least she was talking quietly, so none of the grownups or other kids could hear that she was doubting our story.

"Maybe if we go over the notes," Lenni suggested, "there'll be some way we can prove you were right."

I liked that idea much better than Tina's. We all gathered around Tina as she turned the pages of Casey's notebook. At least that took my mind off all the people in the lobby who were giving us such mean looks.

"I know how we can prove we're telling the truth," I said in a low voice. "We wait until morning. By then, those mannequins will have turned back into wood. People are bound to notice if there's some wooden caveman standing in the middle of Broadway with an ax."

"They'll say we took them and stuck them out there," Gaby muttered.

We went back to studying the casebook. We came to the part about the moccasins with shoelaces. "That's weird," Jamal said. "I've been to this mu-

117

seum loads of times, and I've never seen anything like that."

"Me neither," Alex agreed.

I was looking at Alex in his caveman costume. Then I looked at Tina and Lenni. It was the costumes that finally turned on the lightbulb over my head, as they say. "Wait a minute!" I said. "What if the caveman was wearing a costume?"

"Well, all the mannequins are wearing costumes," said Tina.

"No," Gaby said, catching on to what I was driving at. "Not a permanent costume—more like a disguise."

"And underneath was just some guy," Alex said.

"Who was hiding in the exhibit," said Casey, continuing the thought.

"Now why would someone do that?" asked Lenni.

Tina was flipping through the pages of the casebook. She stopped, flipped back a page. She pointed at a sentence that Casey had underlined. THE GOLD IS REAL.

"How many mannequins did you see come to life with your own eyes?" Alex asked.

"Four," Gaby said.

"Five," I said. "There was the Inuit man."

"There were four," Gaby said, interrupting me. "I didn't see the Inuit come to life."

"Well I did," I said. "He saved our lives."

"Okay," Jamal said, "let's forget about the Inuit

man for a second. What if there were these four robbers—"

"Tomb Robbers!" said Casey.

"Yeah! And they wanted to rob the tomb treasure," I said.

Tina had turned to another page. "In your notes, you say that the museum has all these guards on duty during the day and five guards and all these really fancy burglar alarms at night."

"Right," said Lenni, snapping her fingers. "So they couldn't get the treasure *out* at night."

"What if the robbers hid in the exhibits at the end of the day?" Jamal said. "That way they could steal the stuff at night. Then wait till morning when the alarms are off. Then they change back into their street clothes and walk out of the building with the statues hidden under their coats."

"That's it!" I said. I had been sure that the mannequins were coming to life. Now I was just as sure they were robbers.

We didn't come up with our solution to the mystery a moment too soon. Because just then, Mr. Cepeda, Mr. Fernandez, the two guards, and the cop all walked over to talk to us. They didn't look any less mad than they had a few minutes before.

"Okay," the cop said. "The guards have agreed not to press charges against you for all the trouble you have caused. They're relying on your teacher—"

"And me," said Mr. Fernandez grimly.

"—to punish you severely," Mr. Cepeda finished.

"Mr. Cepeda," I said proudly, "you're probably not going to believe this, but I can explain everything."

"You're right," Mr. Cepeda said. "I don't believe you."

"I know," I said. "But here's the thing. The exhibits weren't coming to life after all."

"Well, what do you know?" said Mr. Cepeda. "I *do* believe you."

"The museum was robbed," I said.

This didn't get the big response I was hoping for. Guard number 4 said, "That's impossible." Guard number 2 agreed.

So then we explained everything we had come up with about the robbers' plan. Guess what? They still didn't believe a word of it.

"Well," Alex said. "There's a simple way we can prove we're right. Let's go look at the pyramid and see if the treasure is still there."

From the look on all the adults' faces, I could tell they weren't in the mood to go anywhere. But they finally agreed. We filed out of the lobby, leaving the rest of the class behind with guard number 2. "Wait here," Mr. Cepeda told them. Which pleased me no end. I was back to feeling like an important person, not like I was about to be thrown in jail.

We were marching through the same halls that

had scared us so bad. But now we had a big group with us, including a policeman.

"Watch out for the rattlesnake," Casey sang out.

Guard number 4 laughed. "This is such nonsense," he said. But I could see he was watching where he was stepping.

When we got to the Tomb Room, the two guards stationed there walked over.

"What's up?" asked one, eyeing us all.

"It's just a bunch of crazy kids making trouble," said guard number 4.

As it turned out, there was no need to go inside the tomb. Guard number 4 lifted a tiny, hidden observation window on the outside of the pyramid. He looked through, then looked at me and smirked.

"Come see for yourself," he said. I did.

The Golden King was still lying in his coffin. So were his ten little sun worshipers, all bowing to the west.

"This is the absolute last straw," Mr. Cepeda said. "Hector, I never would have expected you to behave like this, but let me tell you, the fun and games are totally over, *mi amigo*. You and your friends—"

"Wait a minute!" cried Gaby. "The statues have been switched! And I can prove it!"

chapter
eighteen

"That is so ridiculous I can't even tell you," said guard number 4 with a big sigh. "Those statues look exactly like they always do."

"Not exactly," Gaby said.

Everyone stared at her, waiting.

"Can I see your Caseybook?" Gaby asked Casey.

"Tina's got it."

Tina handed the notebook over to Gaby, who started searching through the pages.

"Well?" asked Mr. Cepeda.

"Just one second," Gaby said, without looking up.

"This had better be good, Gabriella," warned her father.

Please be right, Gaby, I silently begged her. *Whatever it is, please be right.*

"I'm right!" she said. She looked up, grinning.

"The plaque in there says that the sun worshipers greet the rising sun, right?"

"Right," said the two guards.

I said "Right" as well, without even thinking about it.

"And it says those statues were set up that way, to greet the rising sun, right?"

"Right."

"Well there you have it," Gaby said, snapping the casebook shut with a bang.

"There you have *what?*" the cop demanded.

"All over the world, the sun rises in the east, not the west," Gaby explained. "And if you take another look in that little observation window, you'll see that those little gold men are now bowing to the west. Somebody switched them with fake statues. Somebody who was in one big hurry. And they put the fakes back wrong."

Guard number 4 and the policeman rushed to the window to see if Gaby was right. They bumped into each other, trying to get a look. "It's true," said Guard number 4, who was the first one to the window. "The statues have been switched."

His skin had turned toad-belly pale. His little mustache was twitching.

"But how?" continued guard number 4. "We have two guards in this room at all times." He nodded toward the other two guards.

"Not quite all the time," Casey corrected him. She pulled out the schedule. "There's a fifteen-minute gap where there's only one guard."

She smiled at me. I smiled back.

"And the pyramid has those two exits," I said, remembering our hair-raising chase through the pyramid's dark tunnels.

"So," Gaby said, "if there was only one of you in here for fifteen minutes, you couldn't cover both exits. They could have slipped in there without your seeing them."

"No wonder they were in such a rush to get us out of there," Casey said. "They didn't have much time."

Guard number 4 was in a rush as well. He ran to use the phone.

Just then, Lieutenant McQuade ran in, all out of breath. It turned out he had been chasing the robbers all this time. "Did you catch them?" I asked.

He shook his head.

But in a way, it didn't matter, because Lieutenant McQuade could still back up our story. He knew we weren't the ones who attacked the guard.

Fifteen minutes later, an impressive-looking man with a silver beard arrived in the Tomb Room. He looked very sleepy and very upset. Turned out he was John Madison Bell, the director of the entire museum. He looked through the observation window, then he went into the pyramid itself. When he came back out, he looked like he had lost two night's sleep instead of just one.

"I'm afraid these children are correct," he announced in a hushed voice. "We've been robbed. We've lost millions."

At that moment, I probably should have been feeling bad. Four robbers had just made off with the museum's treasure, slipping right through our fingers, too. But that wasn't what I was feeling. I was feeling great. At least now everyone believed us about the mannequins who had come to life. And we weren't in trouble anymore. In fact, we were heroes.

Mr. Cepeda saw that it must have been the robbers who locked them into the Bird Room. He apologized to us over and over. Lieutenant McQuade and Mr. Bell both thanked the whole Ghostwriter Team for alerting them to the robbery. Then Mr. Bell gave us his home phone number. He asked us to call him personally—any time of day or night—if we remembered anything more about the robbers.

Then we went home.

I was dropped off at my apartment around four in the morning. My mom and I have a tiny one-bedroom apartment. I sleep on the living room sofa. My mom was already asleep of course, since she thought I was spending the night at the museum. The only sound was the plop-plop-plop of water still leaking in the living room. Mom had set up a plastic bucket to catch the spill.

I tiptoed around trying not to make a lot of noise. I folded out the sofa bed, changed into my pajamas, and got into bed. But I was totally wired and couldn't sleep. I couldn't even close my eyes.

Alex had given me half his bag of candy, which was really nice of him. So I stayed up, sitting by the window, eating candy and saving the wrappers for my collection. I was looking out at the courtyard and playground in front of the projects. They're all covered with graffiti, but I love them anyway, I guess because they're so familiar. But anyway, that wasn't what I was seeing just then.

I was seeing everything that had happened that night. The scenes kept playing over and over in my mind.

And then I thought of something. I thought of the word *guide*. I thought of how Ghostwriter had found it on the second floor of the museum when we were lost and waiting in the Hall of Minerals and Gems.

And once I thought of that, I kept on thinking of it. It was as if I had a VCR in my brain and someone kept pressing Rewind and running the tape again and again.

I uncapped my Ghostwriter pen. It was five in the morning. I didn't care. I took a piece of paper from next to the phone and wrote, "RALLY H." Ghostwriter flew away with the letters right away, so I guess he wasn't sleeping, either. But nobody answered. So I picked up the phone.

I called Casey first. Except I got Grandma CeCe. It took nine rings, and she sounded groggy and angry. "You better have a very good reason for waking me up," she said.

I apologized and told her it was *muy importante.* "I need to talk to Casey," I said.

Grandma CeCe wanted to have Casey call me back in the morning. She was sure Casey was sleeping. But while she was on the phone, I heard Casey say, "I've got it, Grandma."

The phone klunked down and I heard Mrs. Jenkins muttering, but then Casey came on.

"Hello?" Casey asked.

"I thought of something."

"What?

"Remember when we were lost?"

"No, I already forgot," said Casey.

"Stop joking. I'm serious."

"I remember."

"We were in the Hall of Minerals and Gems," I said. "Ghostwriter found Mr. Cepeda's guide pass, but he found it on the second floor."

"So?"

"So Mr. Cepeda and the class were locked in the Bird Room."

There was a silence. Then Casey said, "O.T.F.F."

"Right," I said.

"You know what I mean?"

"On the First Floor," I said.

Casey giggled. "Okay!" Then she said, "Hey, I wonder what *those* letters stand for? *O* and *K* . . ."

"Casey, don't you see?" I asked.

There was another silence. Then Casey gasped and said, "Wait a minute! Who was the *other* guide?"

"Exactly!"

"What if one of the robbers was a museum guide?" Casey asked.

"That's what I'm thinking. He could have been wearing his street clothes—with his guide pass—*under* his costume."

"Right, right, right!" Casey cried.

I was so excited that Casey agreed with me, I got a little carried away and started talking pretty loud. My mom woke up.

"Hector?" she called from the bedroom. "Why are you back so early, *hijo*?"

Sometimes if I wake up my mom accidentally and she doesn't stay up for long she can go right back to sleep. So I answered her all in one breath. "It's-a-long-story-but-everything's-okay-go-back-to-sleep-I'll-tell-you-all-about-it-tomorrow-morning."

I listened. She was quiet. Then I started talking to Casey in a whisper. "Sorry," I said.

"Hector," she said. "You're a genius."

"Well . . ." I said, reddening.

"I'm serious. You gotta call Mr. Bell. You solved the crime!"

Grandma CeCe started yelling at Casey to get off the phone and go to sleep.

"Should I call him now?" I asked her.

"Definitely," Casey said. "He said to call anytime."

Casey was right, because Mr. Bell answered on the first ring.

"Mr. Bell? This is Hector Carrero, one of the kids tonight at the museum? I hope I'm not waking you up."

"Trust me, you're not."

"Yeah, well, good. Uh, I can't sleep either. And I think I may have come up with something that might help you."

"Are you whispering? I'm having a little trouble hearing you."

"My mom's asleep."

"Ah. Sorry. Please go on."

But I didn't go on. I didn't say a word.

"Hello? Hector?"

I had suddenly realized that my theory was going to be very hard to explain. It was bad enough I had spent the night trying to convince people that the museum's exhibits were coming to life. Now what was I supposed to say? This ghost friend of ours gave me a big clue?

Our team had sworn to keep Ghostwriter a secret. After all, he only talked to us and nobody else. We figured he must have had a good reason for keeping himself hidden, and we respected it.

"Hector?" Mr. Bell asked again.

"Uh . . . it's a little hard to explain."

"Take your time."

"Well, um, my friends and I think that one of the robbers is the museum guide," I said.

"Why?" Mr. Bell asked at once. Which led me right back to the part I didn't know how to explain.

I took a deep breath. "Mr. Bell? You know how we've been right about everything we've told you so far? Well, could you maybe just trust me on what I'm about to say?"

There was a pause. "Okay," he said, sounding unsure.

"Thank you. I think you should question your guide very carefully."

"Which one?"

"Which one what?"

"Which guide is the robber?"

My heart sank. "You mean you have more than one?"

"We have seven full-time guides."

"*Seven?*" My heart went on sinking. Here I thought I had found the robber for sure.

"Well," I said, "just look to see which guide

132

doesn't show up for work tomorrow. Then go find him—or her—and arrest him. Or her."

"Hmm," Mr. Bell said. "I don't know."

"Why not?"

"Well, if you're right, Hector, and this is an inside job, as they say . . . I don't think the guide would skip work tomorrow. It would look too suspicious."

"You're right," I said, disappointed. Maybe I wasn't such a genius after all.

I heard my mother stirring in her bedroom. I waited for a couple of seconds. Then, lowering my voice even further, I said, "Sorry. So now what?"

"Hector," Mr. Bell said, "if you and your friends would be willing to do us yet another favor, I have a plan. . . . "

chapter
nineteen

"Now over here we have the most important and exciting exhibit of all," the guide told us. "The gift shop."

Everyone on the tour laughed. The guide smiled. "No, but seriously, what I like to do is start all my tours in the gift shop. That way, you guys can get all your souvenir-hunting out of your system. Then you can concentrate on my wonderful tour."

It was eleven the next morning. Mr. Bell had asked me and my teammates to go on all the museum tours and see if we could recognize the robber. Since there were seven guides and seven of us, we decided we would each go on a different tour. Then we were going to meet and compare notes. Right now, I was feeling like I was going to have nothing to report.

Our guide was a tall and pretty woman with long brown hair. I kept staring at her, trying to imagine her as an Indian bride. But last night that bride had worn a veil and all I had seen were her brown eyes. This guide had brown eyes; but then, so did a lot of people.

I studied her closely, searching for clues. I looked at her oval face, red lipstick, gold hoop earrings, long blue dress, silver bracelet, turquoise ring, and brown leather pumps. Nothing looked familiar to me. Basically, I figured there was no way for me to know if this was *the* guide.

I was looking through the postcard spin racks in the gift shop when I had an idea. I bought a picture postcard that showed the Indian bride exhibit. I went up to the guide and showed it to her. "Are we going to see this exhibit today? It's my favorite."

The guide glanced at the card, then smiled at me. "Definitely," she said. "It's on the tour."

"Oh, great," I said. I studied her face.

She smiled at me some more. "Did you have another question?"

"Uh, no."

One more smile, then she patted my shoulder. "If you think of anything, just ask."

It couldn't be her, I told myself. No one could be that calm under pressure.

And then the tour began.

"This is the giant squid," our tour guide was telling us. "See how long those tentacles are? They could wrap around your stomach ten times."

I kept watching her face, trying to catch her eye, trying to see if she recognized me or would give me funny looks.

She didn't.

Not once.

By the time we had reached the Caveman Café, which was the second to last stop on the tour, I was pretty depressed. I hadn't found out a single thing.

"Okay," our guide said, clapping her hands. "If I could have your attention for just one moment. The planetarium is our next and final stop on the tour. But first we're going to take a fifteen-minute break here for everybody to fill up their tanks with some yummy museum snacks. May I recommend my personal favorite?" She held up a Museum Munch Bar and bit off a piece. "You can get them in the machines over there. But watch out. I thought I'd have just one. That was two years ago, and I've been having two of these a day ever since."

I wanted to buy a soda, but after traveling back and forth to the museum last night and today, I had spent the last of my allowance on subway tokens. So I just drank and drank out of the bubbler.

Then I sat around feeling glum, watching all the rich tourists stuffing their faces with junk food.

Before we went into the planetarium, the rest of

my team showed up. They had finished their tours. They didn't look any happier than I was.

"Find anything?" I asked Alex out of the side of my mouth, keeping my eyes on my guide.

"Nothing."

From the looks on everybody's faces, I knew that his answer went for the rest of the team as well.

"How about you?" Jamal asked me.

I shook my head.

Our guide opened the doors to the planetarium and led us inside. First we saw this huge model of the solar system. Then we went into this black-light gallery and watched a solar eclipse. But I wasn't too excited. Even outer space was boring compared to catching a thief. And it didn't look like I was going to be doing that anytime soon.

We hung out in the back of the tour group. None of us was paying much attention to what the guide was saying.

"Anyone have any gum?" Lenni asked. "My mouth tastes like a sewer."

I slapped the pocket of my shirt and was surprised to find something in there. I pulled it out. I stared at it, puzzled. Then I realized what it was. I was wearing the same shirt I had worn last night. I was holding the remains of my Museum Munch Bar, which I had eaten down to the letter *C.* So all that remained was—

"Oh wow," I said, staring at the candy bar.

"What?" Tina asked. "It's got ants in it?"

"You okay?" Lenni asked me. "You look like you chipped a tooth."

I didn't look at her. I looked directly at our guide, who was talking about how much we'd weigh on the planet Jupiter. She looked right back at me, too, and gave me another one of those warm smiles.

I smiled right back, trying to make my smile just as warm and friendly and innocent as hers.

And then I said in a whisper to my friends, "She's the one."

c h a p t e r
twenty

We were all filing into the Night Theater. "The Zeiss VI Star Projector magically imitates the night sky," our guide said in a loud voice. "The computer automation system that controls this show is one of the largest in the world. So take your seats and get ready to go on an amazing journey through outer space."

"How do you know it's her?" Jamal asked me. He said it quietly. He was looking straight up at the domed roof of the theater, as if he weren't talking to me at all.

I nudged him and held out my half-eaten candy bar—not all the way up where the guard could see it and a little away from my body. I glanced around at my teammates, saw them all staring at the chocolate candy I held in my hand. The candy with the letters stamped into it.

The remaining letters spelled CH BAR.

"So?" whispered Tina.

I bit off one more section of candy, chewed, then held out what was left.

H BAR.

"That's the clue Ghostwriter read near *guide*," Casey whispered.

Just then the door to the theater opened behind us and Mr. Bell stepped in, along with three security guards. It was dark in the room. I hoped the guide didn't notice them.

Mr. Bell was standing right behind me. I didn't turn around. "Any luck?" he asked us.

"You're looking at one of the four thieves," I said.

"How do you know?"

"Because the thief had a Museum Munch Bar last night, and this guide loves them and eats them every day."

"Hmm," said Mr. Bell, sounding disappointed. Then he took two Museum Munch Bars out of his pocket. "So do I. So does everyone around here. They're delicious."

Back to square one. Luckily, just then I thought of something else. I took out my postcard of the Indian bride exhibit and peered at it in the dark. I counted eight gold bracelets on the bride's wrist. Then I handed the card back to Mr. Bell. "Here's more proof," I said. "She was wearing nine bracelets last night. She forgot to take off her silver bracelet. The one she's wearing right now."

Mr. Bell looked at the postcard, then at the guide. His eyes narrowed.

The guide was looking right back at us. Just then, she clapped her hands, as if she were applauding my detective work. "Okay," she called up to the projection booth. "Let's get this show on the road!"

The lights went off. The laser lights came on. On the dome over our heads thousands of stars began to twinkle and shine. Space-age music blasted over the sound system. I looked back at the guide.

She had vanished.

chapter
twenty-one

"Let's go!" said Lenni.

The team scattered in all directions, running down the theater aisles, trying to find the robber. The guards were running, too. But the guide was nowhere to be found.

I saw Casey scribbling furiously in her Caseybook. I ran to her and looked over her shoulder. She was telling Ghostwriter what was going on. She ended her message by writing, "FIND GUIDE!"

Ghostwriter swept up the letters and zoomed off. I bent my head back and looked straight up, as if the guide might somehow have flown up into that fake sky.

It was a good thing I did.

Because I saw a constellation of stars on the roof glowing brightly. Ghostwriter had connected the dots to spell out P.B.

"Ghostwriter!" I said.

"Who?" said a man who was sitting on the aisle.

"P.B.," said a familiar voice. Gaby was right by my side in the darkness. She too was gazing up at the dome.

"Peanut butter?" I guessed.

And then another familiar voice spoke up behind me. "No," Casey said. "Projection Booth!"

"She's in the projection booth!" I shouted at once, which was how sure I was that Casey had gotten it right.

The guards started climbing up these metal ladders up to the catwalk on either side of the dome. The next thing I knew, there were giant shadows splashing across the sky show.

They must have caught the guide right in front of the projector, because we could see the whole thing. Not knowing what was going on, the crowd oohed and ahead. They seemed to think the arrest was the best part of the show. I had to agree.

I guess I should wrap this story up now. I mean, that's basically everything that happened. Except of course for the most amazing, exciting thing of all.

Which I'll get to in just a second.

First of all, the guide confessed. Turned out she was the mastermind of the whole thing. She named her three partners in crime. So the museum caught all the robbers (thanks to us) and got back their little gold statues.

As a reward, we all got free museum passes, which were good for the whole year. Before last night, I didn't know or care too much about museums, and I would have thought that our reward was P.B. No, not Peanut Butter and not Projection Booth. Pretty Bogus.

But now that I'd been to the museum and after everything that happened, I thought it was W.C. Way Cool.

As we were walking out of the museum with our passes, Casey started giggling up a storm. She whispered to Gaby, who started laughing, too.

"Now what?" I asked them.

" 'Please help us, Mr. Inuit,' " Casey said. She was crying, she was laughing so hard.

And when she explained to the rest of the team how I had talked to the Inuits and even thanked them for the use of their knives and spears, everyone on the team was laughing at me as well.

I wasn't mad. I was stunned. I had forgotten all about that. "Guys," I said. "Don't you see? The legend was really true after all!"

"Don't even try to get out of it," Jamal said, chuckling. "Take it like a man."

"Hey, I would have acted the same way if I had been in your situation," Alex said with a grin.

"No, no no!" I said. "I'm totally serious. The Inuit man was alive. He helped me."

They just laughed harder. I started to get angry. I made them all come back with me to the Inuit exhibit so I could prove it to them.

"Here we go again," Casey said. She was still giggling. I had never liked Casey more than I did last night. But today, that giggling of hers was starting to get right back on my nerves again.

"Hector, you want us to hide underneath the exhibit like last time?" Gaby teased.

Ignoring her, I stared through the glass. There was my friend, looking down at the same fish, just like always. He was frozen in the exact same position as last night. He was still holding his knife. He had turned back into wood.

"Hola, amigo," I said sadly.

"Unbelievable," Tina said. "Hector made friends with a block of lumber."

Mr. Inuit? I said. I didn't say it out loud, because I was feeling foolish enough as it was. And besides, I doubted he could hear me through the glass anyway. *Mr. Inuit, could you do me one last big favor? I know you have to wait till next year before you can come to life again. But could you just do a little something to show my teammates that you're really alive? Like skin the fish a little, maybe?*

The Inuit man didn't move.

My friends were already heading off down the hallway. They were laughing and calling for me to follow.

I was about to follow them when . . .

No one believes what I'm about to say. Everybody claims it was just my wild imagination acting up all over again. Well, I don't care if you believe me or not. I know this happened. I know it's true.

I put my hand on the glass to say good-bye to the Inuit.

And right then . . .

The Inuit man looked up and gave me a wink.

Then he put his head back down again.

I stood there a long time, too stunned to speak.

I looked to see if my teammates had noticed, but they were already way down the hall.

So it would just be my secret.

I could live with that, I thought. And I could live without a week's worth of milk money—I planned to keep my promise to the Inuit and donate it to the museum. I waved good-bye to the Inuit.

And I started down the long hallway after my friends.

COMING SOON FROM GHOSTWRITER!

Look for the next Ghostwriter book, *Movie Marvels: Film Facts You'll Flip For.* It's packed with exciting facts about famous actors, animals in the movies, supercool special effects, directions on how to make a flip action book, and more . . . and it's coming soon to a bookstore near you!

From the
Hit TV Show

Ghostwriter

Created by CTW

GHOSTWRITER—READ IT! SOLVE IT! TELL A FRIEND! CHECK OUT THESE GHOSTWRITER BOOKS.